**"I don't like the way we left things between us,"
Nate declared, taking a step in her direction.**

Mia took a matching step backward. "You asked for
something I couldn't give you."

"I asked for you to come back to Las Vegas with me."

"We'd barely known each other two months." It was the
same excuse she'd given him three weeks ago and it rang
as hollow now as it had then. "And I couldn't leave Ivy."

"She could've found another assistant." He'd said the
same thing the morning after the tour ended. The night
after she'd stayed with him until the sun crested the
horizon.

Their last stop had been Sydney. Following his final
encore, Nate had made sure Ivy was busy and then
stolen Mia away to a romantic hotel suite overlooking
the harbor. They'd sipped champagne, toasted each
other, laughed and made love for the first time. But as
sunlight filled the room, Mia was on the phone with Ivy
making excuses for where she'd been.

"I'm not just her assistant. I'm her sister," Mia said, now
as then. "She needs me."

I need you.

He wouldn't repeat the words. It wouldn't do any good.
She'd still choose obligation to her sister over being
happy with him.

And he couldn't figure out why.

* * *

Little Secret, Red Hot Scandal is part of the
Las Vegas Nights series:

An exclusive club, for men who have it all and want more.

Dear Reader,

I've always been a fan of underdog stories and secret romances, so I thought, *Why not combine the two?* Mia is talented but overshadowed by her sister's star power. That doesn't stop Nate from noticing her.

I absolutely loved their connection. Maybe a little too much. It was hard keeping them apart as I told their story. Thank heavens for Ivy. Her diva ways threw a wrench in the romance between Mia and Nate at every turn.

This was such a fun book to write. I hope you enjoy Mia and Nate's story.

All the best,

Cat Schield

CAT SCHIELD

LITTLE SECRET, RED HOT SCANDAL

HARLEQUIN®DESIRE

Recycling programs
for this product may
not exist in your area.

ISBN-13: 978-0-373-83844-8

Little Secret, Red Hot Scandal

Copyright © 2017 by Catherine Schield

This edition published by arrangement with Harlequin Books S.A.

For questions and comments about the quality of this book, please contact us at CustomerService@Harlequin.com.

Printed in U.S.A.

Cat Schield has been reading and writing romance since high school. Although she graduated from college with a BA in business, her idea of a perfect career was writing books for Harlequin. And now, after winning the Romance Writers of America 2010 Golden Heart® Award for Best Contemporary Series Romance, that dream has come true. Cat lives in Minnesota with her daughter, Emily, and their Burmese cat. When she's not writing sexy, romantic stories for Harlequin Desire, she can be found sailing with friends on the St. Croix River, or in more exotic locales, like the Caribbean and Europe. She loves to hear from readers. Find her at catschield.com and follow her on Twitter, @catschield.

Books by Cat Schield

Harlequin Desire

The Black Sheep's Secret Child
Nanny Makes Three
Two-Week Texas Seduction

The Sherdana Royals

Royal Heirs Required
A Royal Baby Surprise
Secret Child, Royal Scandal

Las Vegas Nights

At Odds with the Heiress
A Merger by Marriage
A Taste of Temptation
Little Secret, Red Hot Scandal

Visit her Author Profile page at Harlequin.com, or catschield.com, for more titles!

For my daughter, who keeps me current on all things pop culture.

One

After telling the sound engineer to take a break, Nate Tucker lay down on the couch in the control room of West Coast Records' LA headquarters. Closing his eyes, he listened to the playback of the song he'd just recorded. Over the years he'd trained his ears to pick up every nuance of a performance. His mind then went to work adjusting the frequencies, boosting or cutting EQ, feathering in a touch of reverb to improve the natural sound.

Nothing, however, could fix what Nate was hearing in his own voice. Proof that he'd pushed too hard on the final leg of his twelve-month tour.

He'd hoped that three weeks of rest might have allowed his vocal cords to fix themselves, but his reduced range and the hoarseness that plagued him weren't going away. The vocal cord surgery he'd scheduled for tomorrow was unavoidable. Nate's curses echoed through the room. One more damned thing he didn't have time for.

Since returning to his home in Las Vegas after touring all over the world with his band, Free Fall, he'd been inundated with work. Thank goodness he'd been able to do some songwriting while on the road, because he was all out of space and energy to compose for Free Fall's next album. Maybe that wasn't such a bad thing. With his voice out of commission he wasn't going to be singing anytime soon.

His phone began to ring. Nate checked the screen before levering himself off the couch. In the last three days he'd made a half dozen calls to Trent Caldwell, his business partner and friend. In addition to being partners in Club T's, the premier Las Vegas nightclub that Nate, Trent and Kyle Tailor owned, Nate and Trent were partners in Nate's label, Ugly Trout Records in Las Vegas, as well as West Coast Records, the company Trent had recently bought from his family.

Dropping into the control booth's comfortable leather chair, Nate silenced the music pouring from the speakers and answered the call.

"It's about time you checked in." Nate wasted no time with pleasantries. "Where have you been?"

"Savannah starts shooting next week, so I took her and Dylan to a spa hotel up in Washington." Trent sounded more relaxed and happy than ever. Being engaged to the love of his life obviously agreed with him. "We both turned off our phones for a few days."

Ever since Trent had rekindled his romance with his former lover and found out he was a father, he'd become a whole new person. Nate understood the transformation, after what had happened between him and Mia. It was easy to be cynical and even suspicious about stuff like that until it happened to you.

"Sounds nice." Really nice.

Envy shot through Nate. It wasn't like him to want something another man had. He already had fame and wealth. They didn't drive him. Nate loved what he did and didn't really care if he made tons of money. The music mattered.

And then he'd watched his friend and business partner fall hard for Savannah, and suddenly making music wasn't enough anymore.

"I got your messages about the meeting with Ivy Bliss," Trent said. "Have you lost your mind?"

"What do you mean?" Nate knew perfectly well what Trent was referring to, but decided to pretend he'd been motivated purely by business.

Ivy Bliss was a former child actress turned pop princess with an impressive four-octave range. Five years ago she'd signed with West Coast Records and released two albums. They'd done okay. Thanks to the label's poor management, the production work on the albums hadn't been stellar and the release dates had been pushed back so many times that fans had lost interest.

That was before Trent and Nate had taken control of his family's label the previous month. They intended to turn the record company around and make it a huge success. Ivy Bliss's new album was a great place to start.

But that wasn't the reason Nate had reached out to Ivy's manager-father about producing her new album.

"You did nothing but complain about her the entire eight weeks she was on tour with you."

"Oh, that."

"Oh, that?" Trent mimicked. Nate could hear a baby babbling in the background. "Just a second." There was a pause. "Dylan, Daddy's on the phone with Uncle Nate. Do you want to sing him your new song?"

Nate couldn't ignore the growing ache in his chest as he listened to Dylan jabber along with his father's soft singing. Ever since Nate had decided on a career in music, every bit of his energy had been focused on writing, performing and producing. Now, he enjoyed all the money and success he'd dreamed about and yet something gnawed at him.

"That was terrific," Nate said when the song was done.

"He's barely a year and already starting to say a few words."

"Have you been teaching him the signs I showed you?" Nate had learned American Sign Language as a kid so he could communicate with his hearing impaired mother, and had taught Trent a few signs Dylan could use to communicate, for words such as *more*, *done*, *eat*, *play*, *finish* and *tired*.

"Yes, he's really taking to it. Now, back to Ivy. Why would you want to produce her new album?"

Nate sighed. "I don't need to remind you that she's a huge talent and poised to break out. She just needs one great album."

"She's a twenty-five-year-old nightmare."

"Yes, well…she's not that bad." Nate winced at the bald lie.

Seven years earlier, when she was seventeen and starring in a Broadway musical after her show on KidZ Channel was canceled, she'd gotten Nate's phone number and for four months she'd sent him impassioned texts and sexy pictures of herself. At first he'd responded with polite rebuffs and then silence. At last he'd contacted her father and warned him that this wasn't going to play well if it got out. All contact stopped.

"She's a little silly and spoiled," Nate continued, "but superstars can get that way sometimes."

Trent ignored his friend's self-deprecating jab. "Why don't you point her toward Savan or Blanco?" Both had worked with her on collaborations with other artists and produced hits.

Nate didn't need to remind Trent that Ivy Bliss had a reputation for being "challenging" in the studio. She didn't take suggestions, and criticism sent her into hysterics. Neither of the producers Trent mentioned would want to work with her again.

"I'm doing this for West Coast Records." Another lie. There were a couple dozen guys who could produce the heck out of Ivy Bliss and make an album that would rocket to the top of the charts.

"I'm not buying it." Trent hadn't made a major success of every one of his business ventures by being dense. "Wait a second, are you into her? Damn. That's crazy, but my sister said you fell for someone on the tour. I never in a million years thought it was Ivy Bliss."

"It wasn't." With a shudder, Nate changed topics before Trent could press further. "The other reason I called is that I'm going in for surgery tomorrow."

"Surgery." Trent's tone sharpened. "What's wrong?"

"I've got these polyps on my vocal cords." He tried to keep the tension out of his voice. The situation was serious, but he didn't want to make a big deal out of it. "I need to get them removed."

"That sounds bad."

"It's outpatient surgery. A couple hours max. I just wanted to let you know that I'm going to be out of commission for a few days."

"Do you want me to take you?"

"And do what?" Nate injected as much sarcasm as he could into the words to hide how embarrassed he was at his mounting anxiety. "Hold my hand? Please."

"Fine." Trent sounded doubtful. "But if you need anything, just let me know."

"Sure."

An hour after hanging up, Nate strode into the conference room for his two o'clock meeting with Ivy Bliss. Only it wasn't Ivy and her manager-father who awaited him, but Mia Navarro, her twin sister and personal assistant. His heart raced across the room toward her. Nate plunged after it for two strides before coming to a stop. What did he think he was going to do? Wrap her in his arms and crush her against his chest? Whisper that the last three weeks had been a living hell without her? That he ached to hear her voice and sulked without her smile to brighten his day?

She'd made her choice and it hadn't been him.

"How have you been?" He searched her face for some sign she'd suffered as he had, lingering over the circles under her eyes and the downward turn of her mouth. To his relief she didn't look happy, but that didn't stop her from putting on a show.

"Things have been great. Ivy's been busy with appearances on *The Tonight Show* and *Ellen*. She's stoked about being asked to perform at the AMAs on the twentieth. And of course she's really excited about working with you."

Nate reined in his impatience, unable to believe that he was nearly back to square one with Mia. He'd spent weeks chatting her up on the tour, afraid if he pushed too fast that she'd retreat into the persona of personal assistant to Ivy Bliss. Many times he'd asked himself why he was working so hard to draw out someone who didn't want to be noticed. Then she'd smile at him and make his entire day.

If only he could convince her to leave Ivy… Mia had more to offer the world than just being her famous sister's flunky. For one thing, she was a ridiculously talented songwriter. When he'd discovered that she had written all the songs her sister had recorded and that she'd been denied credit on the albums, he'd been seconds away from storming into Ivy's hotel room and demanding she go public with the truth.

Mia had been mortified. She'd claimed to be okay with the lies and Nate could understand letting the error stand for the first album, but not the subsequent one. As someone who nurtured artists, he'd been appalled by what had been done to Mia by her own family, and saddened by how she'd been bullied.

"I didn't ask how your sister is doing. I asked about you."

"I'm fine. Never better." Mia could go on for hours talking about Ivy, but when it came to talking about herself, she was fond of two-word sentences.

"Tell me the truth." He was asking after her welfare, but what he really wanted to know was if she'd missed him at all. It seemed crazy that he'd known her for less than three months and in that time she'd become like breathing to him.

"I'm great. Really."

"What have you been doing since the tour ended?"

Mia shrugged. "The usual."

Meaning whatever occupied Ivy was what Mia had been doing. As her sister's personal assistant, she lived and breathed Ivy Bliss, pop princess.

"I hope she gave you a little time off."

"Ivy was invited to a charity event in South Beach and we extended our stay a couple days to kick back and soak up some sun."

Ivy demanded all Mia's time and energy. That Nate had been able to spend any time at all alone with Mia during Ivy's eight-week stint on his tour was nothing short of amazing. They'd sneaked around like teenage kids. The danger of getting caught had promoted intimacy. And at first, Nate had found the subterfuge amusing. It got old fast.

For a while Nate wondered if he'd initially been drawn to Mia because he felt compelled to rescue her from her sister's clutches. When Mia was around Ivy, she was a quiet mouse in the corner, fetching herbal tea, being ready with Ivy's favorite snack, loosening her tension with a quick shoulder massage. And it had bothered Nate that Ivy treated Mia like an employee instead of a sister. She never seemed to appreciate how Mia's kind and thoughtful behavior went above and beyond the role of personal assistant.

"I don't like the way we left things between us," Nate declared, taking a step in her direction.

Mia took a matching step backward. "You asked for something I couldn't give you."

"I asked you to come with me to Las Vegas. I wanted to spend more time getting to know you."

"It was all happening was too fast. We'd barely known each other two months." She'd delivered the same excuse three weeks ago and it rang as hollow now as it had then. "And I couldn't leave Ivy."

"She could've found another assistant." He'd said the same thing the morning after the tour ended. The night after she'd stayed with him until the sun crested the horizon.

Their last stop had been Sydney. Following his final encore, Nate had made sure Ivy was busy and then stolen Mia away to a romantic hotel suite overlooking the harbor. They'd sipped champagne, toasted each other, laughed and made love for the first time. But as sunlight filled the room Mia was on the phone with Ivy, making excuses for where she'd been.

"I'm not just her assistant, I'm her sister," Mia said, now as then. "She needs me."

I need you.

He wouldn't repeat the words. It wouldn't do any good. She'd still choose obligation to her sister over being happy with him. And he couldn't figure out why.

"Your sister is a spoiled brat." Frustration and impatience got the better of him. "The only reason I agreed to work on her album is because of you."

Mia's beautiful brown eyes went round with

shock, and although her mouth dropped open, no words emerged.

Her phone rang, interrupting the heavy silence between them. "It's Ivy." She looked almost relieved by the interruption. "I should get this."

Nate had grown weary of her sister coming between them. He crossed his arms over his chest and let sarcasm slide into his tone. "By all means, take it."

To his surprise, she put the phone on speaker. "Hey Ivy, I'm with Nate right now and you're on speaker."

After a short pause, Ivy's soprano voice came over the line. "Hi, Nate. Has Mia apologized for me missing the meeting and asked if you could meet for a drink later to chat about my album?"

Mia winced and wouldn't meet his gaze.

"Not yet," he answered.

"Then I'll ask." He could hear the seductive pout in Ivy's tone. "Please come by my house at eight."

He understood the invitation for what it was and barely restrained a growl. "If you wanted to talk about your album, you should've come by today."

Mia's large dark eyes went round with concern. *"Don't upset her,"* she told him in sign language.

Nate pretended that he hadn't seen the plea. While on tour they'd discovered they both knew how to sign. Something he'd used to overcome her reluctance to talk to him. That they'd shared a secret language had drawn them together.

"Didn't Mia explain that I had a conflict? I'm meeting with a representative for Mayfair Cosmetics. It's all hush-hush, but they're looking for the new face to represent their beauty line."

"Can you meet for dinner?" Mia signed, her eyes worried.

Nate reined in his temper, reminding himself the reason he'd offered to work with Ivy was so he could spend time with Mia and hopefully convince her to pick him over her sister this time.

"How about I make a reservation for dinner at eight," Nate said.

"Sure. Dinner would be wonderful."

"I'll text Mia with the details and this time you'd better show up." While Mia stared at him in horror, Nate reached out and disconnected the call. "Studio time costs money. I have a dozen artists I'm currently working with. If Ivy's not going to show up ready to work, then she needs to find a different producer for her album."

"Oh, no, please. She's counting on working with you." Mia was breathless and anxious. "I'll make sure she's where she needs to be exactly when you say."

"Promise?"

He held out his hand, impatient to revisit the feel of her. From the first Mia had appealed to him. She was as natural and competent as Ivy was artificial and flighty. But it was that electric charge that sizzled through him when they touched that he craved.

Her eyes were solemn and earnest as she placed her palm against his. "Promise."

Mia hoped Nate wouldn't notice the way her fingers trembled as they shook hands. In those delightful seconds, Ivy Bliss faded from Mia's mind. There was only this tall, charismatic man with eyes the color of storm clouds.

For as far back as she could remember, Mia had been invisible. Why would anyone pay attention to the ordinary-looking child standing beside and a little behind the beautiful, charismatic, talented Ivy? And the difference between the twins had only intensified when Ivy had gotten a role in a television series and gone on to Broadway and a pop music career. Mia had become the quiet shadow at her elbow.

And then she'd met Nate. Never in a million years could Mia have believed that someone as talented and charismatic as the lead singer of Free Fall would notice she existed, much less be attracted to her. He'd seen her as a distinct individual with interests and goals. That was pretty heady stuff. No wonder she'd tumbled head over heels for him. What woman with a pulse wouldn't have?

Then the tour ended and the real world overcame the fantasy one she'd dwelled in for two months. She'd had no choice but to turn down his offer to go with him to Las Vegas. Nate had been so angry with her that last morning in Sydney. He'd accused her of leading him on. It struck her as impossible that a nobody like her could be anything more than a momentary distraction to someone as incredible as Nate Tucker.

Given all that he'd accomplished in the music industry, it amazed Mia that he was only thirty-one. An accomplished singer/songwriter and producer, he'd had six Grammy nominations for producing and won two. His band had been nominated for twenty-nine assorted awards and won eight, including several Grammys and an AMA award for favorite pop/rock band/duo/group.

"Are you okay?" he asked, peering at her.

They were still holding hands. Mia's cheeks heated as she released her grip. "Sorry." She took an awkward step back and bumped into one of the chairs surrounding the large oval conference table. "I was just thinking how lucky Ivy was for getting to work with you."

The dimple flashing in Nate's scruffy cheek vanished. "Mia, about what happened in Sydney—"

"You don't need to go there," Mia said, forcing lightness into her voice. "It was a crazy tour. So much fun. I won't ever forget it."

"That's not what I meant and you know it."

"Please, Nate." She longed to surrender to the intense glow in his eyes and fall into his arms. "You need to focus on Ivy. And so do I. She's really freaked out about this new direction in her career. I told her you were the best producer in the business and that together you would make platinum."

"I couldn't care less about her or her album. I'm only doing this so I can spend more time with you."

His words sent a spear of yearning through her, but Mia shook her head. "Don't say that. Ivy needs this album to be great." Maybe if she had a hit Ivy's insecurity would stop consuming her, and Mia could begin to live her life far from her demanding twin.

"How long are you planning to keep on being her lackey? Don't you want to be free to explore what makes you happy?"

"Of course." And she would have that life if Ivy's new project catapulted her into the big time. "And someday I'll have that chance."

"For your sake I hope someday is soon." The intensity in Nate's gaze made her shiver.

"I have to get going," Mia said, although now that she'd seen Nate again, the last thing she wanted to do was leave. "You'll text me the details about dinner tonight?"

"Yes."

As Nate escorted Mia to the lobby, she noticed he didn't touch her again.

"It was good seeing you," she murmured awkwardly. She wanted to throw herself into his arms and declare how much she'd missed him. But that would only make the problems between them worse.

Mia maintained a firm grip on her impulses. The connection they'd share on tour had been packed up and put away with the instruments, lights and sound equipment. Sneaking around behind Ivy's back had been necessary and exciting, but it wasn't something Mia intended to do any longer.

While on tour Ivy had been distracted by the traveling, flirting with Free Fall's single band members and blowing up social media for her fans. In Las Vegas, she would be completely focused on her music and on Nate. Mia wouldn't have any opportunities for time alone with him.

Ever since Ivy learned that she was going to work with Nate, she'd been more agitated and demanding than Mia ever remembered her being. Mia wasn't a fool. She understood why Ivy was so reluctant to give her space. Heaven forbid Mia would get a life and walk away.

After leaving Nate, Mia was halfway through the errands she was running for Ivy when her phone began to play Ivy's latest hit, her special ring tone. Mia held off answering for several seconds. But she'd already ignored a bunch of Ivy's texts, and her sister would have a fit if she didn't pick up now.

"OMG. Where have you been? I've texted you, like, a dozen times." Ivy's voice poured from Mia's smartphone, scattering her thoughts to the wind. Behind closed doors the sweetheart pop star became a demanding diva. "I've been dying to hear all about how excited Nate is that we're working together."

"Sorry I didn't respond." In fact, she'd been lost in thought and hadn't heard the alerts. "Traffic was crazy and there was an accident…"

"If you were sitting in traffic you should have

called." Ivy barely gave that a second to sink in before continuing, "Whatever. Tell me. Tell me."

"Of course he's excited to be working with you."

"What did he say exactly?"

"That you're going to make the best album ever."
It was lame, but her sister would freak if Mia shared
what Nate had actually said. "But listen, Ivy—"

Her sister's squeal interrupted her. "I knew it. He
is into me."

"I'm sorry. What?" Mia almost rear-ended the car
in front of her when the driver stopped abruptly to
avoid hitting an SUV that cut him off.

"Nate. He's into me." Ivy sounded quite pleased
with herself. "I told you how he was hitting on me
on tour."

"Nate hit on you?" Mia's stomach clenched in dismay at Ivy's words. "When was that?"

When it came to her sister, Mia was like one of
Pavlov's dogs. She panicked at the first sign that her
sister was scheming. Ivy made an art form out of
keeping the focus on her. Even before Ivy became
famous she knew how to manipulate a situation to
suit her and often Mia received the full brunt of the
backlash. Since then Ivy had pulled several stunts
to stay in the spotlight. Mia had learned to keep her
head down.

"All the time. How did you not notice?"

"Sure. Of course." Mia was glad her sister couldn't
see her expression.

"And I never told you, but that last night in Sydney…" She let the confession hang in the air to build suspense.

"What about it?"

"We were together."

A curse shot from Mia before she could stop herself. "Sorry, I almost hit the car in front of me. This traffic is—"

"Whatever. Did you hear what I said?"

"About you being with Nate that last night in Sydney?" Mia was torn between a laugh and a groan. Good thing she'd already put her romance with Nate behind her. Now that Ivy had decided she wanted him, any hint that Mia had feelings for him would be disastrous.

"I should've told you."

Mia's voice was uncharacteristically sharp as she asked, "Why didn't you?"

"You don't need to be such a bitch. I'm sorry I didn't say something sooner, but I wasn't sure if what we had was going anywhere."

"And now?" Mia turned into the parking structure closest to the stores she needed to hit.

"Ever since I found out he asked to work with me on my new album, I've been convinced what we have is the real deal." Ivy sounded at the same time dreamy and triumphant. "When will you be getting back to the house?"

"I'm heading to Rodeo Drive to take care of the stuff you wanted me to return." Ivy loved to shop, but she could be fickle when it came to liking things once she got them home. "It shouldn't take me more than half an hour."

As self-absorbed as Ivy could be, when it came to her twin, she liked knowing everything Mia was up to. It had gotten to the point where Mia gave up on having secrets of her own. Or that's the way it had been until Nate came along. That they shared the ability to sign had enabled Mia to have something all to herself that Ivy couldn't barge in on and take over.

Mia realized she'd been counting on this album to launch her sister, hoping that it would be enough of a distraction to allow Mia to escape.

Was that how she viewed Ivy? As someone Mia needed to run away from? The relationship between Mia and her sister hadn't always been so strained. Until the last three or four years, when Ivy's career really took off, Mia and Ivy had been as close as two people who shared the same womb for nine months could be.

If anything demonstrated how much Mia craved a chance to get out of Ivy's shadow, it was her clandestine flirtation with a man her sister had shown an interest in. And now Mia realized that despite the way she'd left things that last morning in Sydney, a part of her hadn't given up on pursing a relationship with Nate.

In the beginning she'd simply enjoyed Nate's charismatic presence. Not only was the lead singer of Free Fall a musical genius, he had killer dimples that rendered her speechless, and the sort of lean muscles that made her all too aware of her vulnerable heart, unsteady knees and tendency to blush.

At first she hadn't taken his attention seriously. Fate had seen to it that Ivy was granted all the beauty and most of the talent. Most people outside their family didn't even know Mia and Ivy were sisters, much less twins. Ivy had taken their mother's maiden name because she liked the way it sounded, and Bliss worked great for marketing.

And then one day Nate had been backstage while Ivy rehearsed. She'd stopped the sound check and was shrieking at the drummer for messing with the tempo. Across the ten feet separating them, Mia saw the gesture Nate made, and amusement must have shown on her face because he snagged her gaze and winked.

Mia had signed, asking him if he knew what that particular gesture meant, and he signed back that he absolutely did. For the duration of Ivy's sound check, they'd discovered through sign language that each had a hearing-impaired family member. That day something unexpected had happened to Mia. She'd made an unlikely friend. And in the weeks that followed, it became more.

Ivy broke into her thoughts. "Can you stop and get me a coffee on your way back? You know how I like it."

Keeping up with Ivy's demands required Mia's full attention. For most of her life that hadn't bothered her. But ever since Nate had come along and actually noticed her, not as Ivy's twin or her assistant, but as a desirable woman, Mia spent more and more time thinking about a life away from Ivy.

"Sure." Now all she needed to do was find a way to explain to her family that she wanted to strike out on her own. And that was not going to be easy. "I know exactly how it needs to be."

Two

As soon as Mia left the studio, Nate got on the phone with Trent's sister. Melody had been on the tour with him as the opening act for Free Fall the entire twelve months.

Because he knew her as not only a fantastic songwriter and singer, but also as the little sister of his best friend and business partner, when she'd asked what was going on between him and Mia, he'd told her. Melody didn't like the way Mia was treated by her sister any more than he did. She'd grown up with a father who liked to bully people and had a particular sensitivity to such treatment.

Once she'd been clued in to what was going on, Melody had helped keep Ivy distracted so Nate and Mia could have as much uninterrupted time together as possible. At first Nate wasn't sure if Mia had any idea how Melody was helping them, but she'd caught on quickly. Mia and Melody shared a talent for songwriting and during the hours they spent collaborating became good friends.

The difference in Mia when Ivy wasn't around showed Nate how unhappy Mia was being her sister's personal assistant. Yet whenever he broached the subject of leaving her sister's employment to do something for herself, he hit a brick wall.

"You told your brother I met someone while on tour?"

"I might have mentioned that you were a bit distracted." Melody responded carefully, but there was laughter in her tone.

Nate closed his eyes and rubbed his temple. Melody had a romantic nature and succumbed easily to simple gestures of affection, like the dozen handwritten notes her boyfriend, Kyle Tailor, had tucked amongst the clothes in her suitcase. She'd discovered them halfway across the country and been over the moon that Kyle had done something so romantic.

Unfortunately, the strain of separation for so many months had led to trouble in their relationship. Nate blamed himself. If it weren't for him, Melody never would've gone on tour. He'd been the one who persuaded her to leave behind the anonymity of songwriting and to join him onstage. She had a fantastic voice and deserved to shine.

Fortunately, Kyle didn't blame him. If he had, it

might have put a strain on their business partnership in Club T's.

"He thinks it's Ivy." Nate spent the next minute listening to Melody's laughter. "It's not funny."

"Oh, it is. Why does he think that?"

"Because I suggested I produce her next album. It's the only way I could think of to spend more time with Mia. She's determined we're over."

"I think that's fantastic. The girl has a killer voice and needs a producer who can showcase it. Besides, no one but you can stand up to that father of hers and make sure her next album kills it."

"I'm flattered that you think so." Nate's tone was as dry as the Mohave Desert.

"So how did the meeting go?"

"It didn't. Mia showed up without her sister and father. Apparently they were taking a meeting with someone from Mayfair Cosmetics. They're considering Ivy as their next spokesmodel."

"Are you kidding? They stood you up? Don't they realize who you are?"

"Obviously someone they can skip a meeting with." Nate thought about his stern words to Mia about her sister and regretted taking his frustration out on her. It wasn't her fault how her sister and father behaved. "I'm taking them to dinner tonight. Hopefully, they'll show up this time. I'm going to be out of commission for a few weeks starting tomorrow."

"Out of commission? What's going on?"

"I'm going in for surgery on my vocal cords."

"What? When did this come up?"

"I started noticing a problem on the tour, but we were so close to the end, and I didn't want to cancel any shows." In part because to do so meant shortening his time with Mia. Their relationship heated up a lot in the last two weeks and he wouldn't have missed that for anything.

"This is serious. Why didn't you say anything to me? Does Trent know?"

"I told him earlier today."

"Is he taking you to the surgery appointment?"

"He's out of town. I have a car scheduled. It'll be fine."

"No it won't. I'll get on a plane and be there to take you back to the hotel."

"That's not necessary. You need to stay in Vegas and work on your album. I've given you a deadline, remember?"

"A couple days isn't going to matter one way or another."

"Humor me." Letting anyone baby him was not in his nature. "It's outpatient surgery. I'll be in and out in a few hours."

"Why do you have to be so strong all the time? It wouldn't kill you to accept help once in a while." Melody let loose an exasperated sigh. "You are so stubborn."

After a childhood spent bouncing from one backwater town to another, Nate had learned to take care of himself. Sometimes his dad would be gone for months, sent all over the country to whatever oil fields needed his expertise the most. If the job required an extended stay, he might bring Nate and his mom along. Nate's dad never cared if this meant his son had to fit in at a new school or that his wife would have to take whatever job she could to make ends meet.

"I could say the same of you." Nate knew of only one way to get Melody off this particular subject. "How are things between you and Kyle? Have you talked yet?"

"Did you know that Trent hired Hunter to DJ twice a month at Club T's?"

"He mentioned something about it. I told him it was a bad idea."

Hunter Graves was Melody's ex-boyfriend. Several months ago he and Melody had run into each other in a New York City club. As they were leaving, to keep from getting separated while passing through the raucous crowd outside, Hunter had taken Melody's hand as they headed to a waiting car. The paparazzi had snapped several pictures of the couple and the media had ruthlessly promoted its theory that the former lovers had reunited.

Back home, while Kyle hadn't really believed Melody was cheating on him, he hadn't appreciated seeing the woman he loved hand in hand with her ex. And the months of separation had created tension for the couple, making Kyle even more reactive.

Melody sighed in Nate's ear. "And to answer your earlier question, Kyle and I have exchanged several texts, but we haven't sat down to talk."

"Don't you think that should happen soon?"

"I'm afraid if we have the talk we'll just end up fighting and the subject of us being over will come up."

"Kyle hasn't come to Las Vegas and taken over temporary management of Club T's because he's ready to give up on you two."

"He's here because Trent's in LA with Savannah and the club needs a manager." Melody's voice had a ragged quality that tore at Nate's heart. "Sorry," she muttered. "I really hope you're right about him, but I can't stop feeling like he's going to use what's happened between us since that photo came out to rationalize that we're not really meant to be together."

"He's not going to do that," Nate said. "Especially after he finds out what's really going on."

"What do you mean by that?" Melody sounded more wary than confused.

"You forget how hard it is to keep secrets on tours."

"You and Mia managed."

"That's because the only one we had to keep in the dark was Ivy, and in general she's so preoccupied with herself that she isn't sensitive to what's going on around her." Nate circled back to Melody's problem. "When are you going to tell Kyle he's going to be a father?"

"Damn. Who else knows?"

"Both Dan and Mike commented that you were looking a bit off and mentioned that their wives had both been sick like that when they were pregnant."

"Why did they tell you?"

"Because you're like my little sister and I've made it pretty clear all along that anyone who messed with you would get their ass kicked by me."

Melody huffed out of a breath. "I can take care of myself."

"Aww, that's cute," he mocked. "But you really can't. You are too sweet for your own good and people take advantage of that."

The same could be said of Mia. And his mother. Nate recognized he had a pattern when it came to women. He didn't actively seek out those most in need of protecting, but he did tend to gravitate to the ones who had a hard time sticking up for themselves.

"And you don't let anyone take care of you," Melody countered. "Case in point, tomorrow's surgery."

"Okay, we've both poked at each other's shortcomings long enough," Nate said with a laugh. "I'll shoot you a text tomorrow after it's done and let you know how it went."

"I'm not kidding about coming to LA to sit at your bedside."

"And I appreciate the offer, but I'd rather you take care of things there." He paused before delivering his final bit of advice. "Talk to Kyle. He's going to be thrilled."

"I will. Good luck tomorrow."

"Thanks."

After talking with Melody, Nate made a reservation for four at WP24, Wolfgang Puck's contemporary Asian restaurant on the twenty-fourth floor of the Ritz-Carlton. He selected this particular restaurant knowing Mia would love the downtown LA views and the blackberry soufflé with key lime ice cream for dessert. Once that was done, he texted her the details and then headed to grab a late lunch with his former buddy whose music career had nosedived six years ago, thanks to a drug problem, but who was making a small comeback.

Nate didn't return to his hotel until nearly six. He spent the time before dinner Skyping with his mother and letting her know in rapid ASL about the surgery the following day. At least he wouldn't have to worry about being able to communicate with her over the next two to three weeks while he was on total voice rest. If only the rest of his clients understood sign language, he might be able to maintain his work schedule with barely a hitch.

At a little before eight, Nate stepped off the elevator on the twenty-fourth floor of the Ritz-Carlton and approached the hostess. His pulse kicked up as he looked around for Mia, but he didn't see her or her family. The hostess confirmed they'd not yet arrived, and escorted him to a table by the windows. When the waiter arrived, Nate ordered a vodka on the rocks with a twist of lime. Normally he'd wait until his party showed up, but he expected Mia and her family to be late and they didn't disappoint them. What he hadn't expected, however, was Mia's absence.

Nate stood as Ivy approached. She wore a strapless emerald dress that clung to her slim body and brought out the gold flecks in her brown eyes. Her five-inch heels put a sexy sway in her stride.

"Nate," she cried in delight as if they were the best of friends. "It's so wonderful to see you."

They hadn't gotten along particularly well on the tour. She'd made demands on everyone from the roadies to the tour manager, and some of her requests had been ridiculous. The amount of time Nate had spent running interference hadn't sat well with him. And he had a particular distaste for how she treated Mia.

"Hello, Ivy," he said, pushing down his annoyance at how he'd been stood up earlier. "Good evening, Javier." He reached out his hand to Ivy's father, a handsome dark-haired man trailing in the pop star's wake. One member of the party was missing. "I made the reservation for four. Will Mia be joining us?"

Ivy settled into the chair beside his. "She wanted to come, but what's the point?"

The annoyance that flared in his gut was familiar. Everything about this spoiled narcissistic brat made him long to hand off her album project to another producer, but his whole purpose in working with Ivy was to have time with Mia.

"The point is I invited her."

"I thought the point of this meeting tonight was to discuss Ivy's album," Javier said, coming down on his daughter's side. "Mia's presence is unnecessary."

"Of course." Giving in was exceedingly painful. Nate could only imagine the conversation that had kept Mia away, and his heart ached that she'd received yet another slight from the people who should have had her best interests in mind.

The waiter approached before Nate could say anything more. Ivy ordered champagne and Javier ordered a gin and tonic.

"I've heard the food here is quite good," Javier said.

Ivy rolled her eyes. "If you like Asian."

Nate was pretty certain no matter which restaurant he'd chosen Ivy would've found something wrong with it.

Without Mia's presence, Nate had no desire to linger over the meal. As soon as they'd ordered he cut straight to business. "I have some ideas for how to proceed with your new album."

"I want to go in a completely different direction," Ivy said, cutting him off before she even heard what he had to say. "I'm not going to write my own music this time. I'd like to record some of Melody Caldwell's music. I heard what she was working on during the tour and I think it suits me."

While Nate agreed, he was dismayed that Ivy had no plans to record her sister's songs. Few people knew Ivy didn't write any of her own music but claimed credit for what Mia composed. Nate had discovered this during the tour and couldn't believe Mia let her sister get away with it. He suspected that part of the reason Mia stayed with Ivy and acted as her assistant was to have her music heard by millions. Did Mia know that Ivy was cutting her out? Would this at last be the catalyst that encouraged Mia to sever the bonds with her sister and strike out on her own?

"I can see if Melody would be open to working with you."

"Why wouldn't she?" Javier demanded. "Having Ivy Bliss record her songs would be a good career move for her."

"Currently Melody is working on an album of her own. A song list hasn't been finalized and I can't promise what will be available for you until that happens."

"I have several songs I'm interested in. I'll have Mia send her a list in the morning. I'm sure Melody will understand that I can do them justice."

"Perhaps you and Melody could collaborate on some new stuff," Nate suggested, hoping the offer made Ivy squirm. "I've worked with her on several songs she's recorded. I think you two would enjoy collaborating."

He smiled through the patent lie. If Melody caught wind of what he'd just offered, she'd probably kill him. Nate doubted anyone on the planet enjoyed working with Ivy Bliss.

"I'm afraid my daughter will be too busy to write

any music this year. This afternoon she signed a deal to become the new face of Mayfair Cosmetics. This will entail many media appearances beginning a month from now. We'd like to get in and get her album recorded as soon as possible."

So they expected him to clear his schedule? Nate wasn't surprised. And he would not be bullied. "I'm afraid the next month will not be good for me. Let's look at something after the first of the year?"

"Ivy is doing a movie in January."

Once again Nate reminded himself that the reason he'd agreed to produce the album was to have time with Mia. And then something occurred to him. It was brilliant, and he kicked himself for not coming up with it sooner.

His lips slid into a genuine smile. "Perhaps we could work something out. I'll need to rearrange my schedule and would appreciate having Mia's help to pull it off."

"Mia's help?" Ivy frowned. "What could she possibly do for you?"

"She understands sign language, doesn't she? I could use her as a translator."

Javier frowned. "A translator?"

"I'm going in for vocal cord surgery tomorrow and won't be able to speak for at least three weeks. I can sign and Mia can relay my instructions."

"Couldn't you find someone else to help with that?" Ivy demanded. "An actual interpreter?"

No one else but Mia would do. "Mia knows the music industry and will understand what I'm saying."

"Daddy?" Ivy's dismay was palpable.

Nate fixed Javier with a flat stare. "Surely you can spare her for a month if it means getting Ivy's album done."

Javier glanced at his daughter. "W-well," he stammered. "Of course. If that's what we need to do."

Nate gave a satisfied nod. "It absolutely is."

Mia sat in a chair beside the window of her bedroom in Ivy's house and stared at the front lawn. An hour earlier she'd watched her father's Mercedes retreat down the driveway, and still couldn't believe that she'd been forced to stay behind. More than ever her role as Ivy's personal assistant grated on her.

Though Mia felt trapped by her responsibility to Ivy, she knew that her sister carried an even heavier burden: the weight of their parents' expectations. Mia barely remembered a time when her sister didn't sing. She recalled their modest house in San Diego, where the twins had shared a bedroom with their older sister, Eva. Their mother had homeschooled all three girls, which offered the flexibility for Ivy to audition anytime an opportunity presented itself. And their parents were able to buy a bigger house when Ivy signed a contract for a new TV show on the KidZ Channel. While she wasn't the star, in the show's four-year run Ivy had demonstrated star potential, which had led to her landing a role in a Broadway musical and eventually a record deal with West Coast Records.

With each rise in her career, the family home got bigger and better. Their father had quit his job with the post office to manage Ivy when she signed with KidZ Channel. Ivy became his whole focus.

Which brought Mia to tonight, and the business meeting her father and sister were attending with Nate. And just as her presence hadn't been needed at the Mayfair Cosmetics meeting earlier that day, Mia wasn't included now.

She wondered if Nate's choice of WP24 had been for her benefit. She'd mentioned how she'd always wanted to try the restaurant, but that had been a couple months ago. Had Nate remembered?

Mia's stomach grumbled, reminding her she hadn't eaten anything since noon. Even though her appetite was nonexistent, her body still needed fuel. Time to stop brooding and scrounge up something for dinner. Ivy's housekeeper usually cooked some chicken in case Ivy felt like supplementing her junk food diet with something healthy.

After pulling out the fixings for a salad and chopping up a chicken breast, Mia splurged with an extra tablespoon of ranch dressing. Too bad she gained weight simply by looking at French fries. As she headed into the den to watch some TV and hopefully take her mind off what was going on at WP24, she reminded herself that Nate had appreciated her full breasts, small waist and round hips.

Both Mia and Eva took after their mother with their dark brown hair and eyes, pale skin and curvy bodies. Ivy was built like their dad, lean and sinewy, but she had their mother's hazel eyes, smoldering charm and singing ability. Sharon Bliss had been an opera singer in her youth, but happily traded a career on the stage for being a wife and mother when she got pregnant with Eva.

Mia had barely sat down when her cell phone rang. She smiled when she saw that the caller was Melody. "I feel as if I haven't talked to you in ages. How are you doing?" she said by way of greeting.

"I'm doing great. Working on my album."

"How many songs are you up to now?"

Melody was a prolific songwriter with a powerful voice and distaste for the spotlight. The two women had become close while on tour. Mia didn't realize how much she missed having a friend until she and Melody had clicked.

"I don't know," Melody said. "Maybe around fifty. They're not all good, but many of my favorites are the ones with the biggest flaws. How am I supposed to choose between them?"

"I know the feeling. Some of my best stuff will never be heard." Until she'd gone on tour, only her family knew that she—and not Ivy—was the author of Ivy's hit tunes. Then she'd met Nate and Melody, and both of them had figured out her secret. Or maybe she hadn't tried very hard to conceal it. Both were such talented songwriters that Mia couldn't resist the urge to talk to them about their process.

To preserve the illusion that Ivy was writing her own songs, Mia was always careful to work when no one was around. But sometimes a tune got into her head and she caught herself humming it. The same thing happened with lyrics. It was why she always carried around her journal.

The notebook contained bits and pieces of songs and snippets of lyrics. It also included doodles and miscellaneous thoughts. She filled one every six months or so.

"Nate could help you with that. I'm sure he'd be happy to work up some demos with you that you could shop around the industry. You never know what might get picked up."

"Actually, he's already offered."

"And what are you waiting for?"

Mia hadn't explained to anyone the real reason she stayed at her sister's side despite the way she was treated like hired help instead of family. It wasn't Mia's story to tell and she knew neither Ivy nor her parents would appreciate the information getting out. Not that Melody or Nate couldn't be trusted with yet another of her secrets.

"I'm not waiting for anything. It's just that I barely have enough time to write, much less create demos." But with Ivy scheduled to record her album at Nate's Ugly Trout studios in Las Vegas, perhaps she would have time to do something for herself for a change.

"Speaking of Nate, did you know he was going in for throat surgery tomorrow?"

"No." Mia's heart gave a worried thump. "I knew he was struggling while we were on tour, and that he pushed through because he didn't want to cancel any shows, but we haven't spoken much since the tour ended."

Nate had made it perfectly clear that he wanted to continue the relationship. As intoxicating as their affair had been, Mia knew it was only a matter of time until their paths diverged. He wanted her to choose him over Ivy, but she just couldn't leave her sister. Would the time ever be right? It was the question Nate had posed that last morning in Sydney. Mia had no clear answer.

"I'm worried about him. He's using a car service to get to and from the doctor's office tomorrow, and he doesn't have anyone staying with him at the hotel to help him after the procedure. I was wondering, since you are in LA, if you could check on him."

"Of course." It was something a friend would do and they'd parted on reasonably good terms. Why hadn't he said anything to her when they'd met earlier?

Mia ran through what she would say to her sister tomorrow about taking care of Nate, and decided she would simply tell her that she needed some time off. It wasn't as if Mia got to take vacations like a regular person. All the time she spent around Ivy was work, even when she was technically off. They might head to the Caribbean or the beaches of Europe together for a little R & R, but it wasn't as though Mia got to party all night, drink too much and sleep in.

"Do you know what clinic he's going to?" Mia asked. "And what time the surgery is?"

"No. I'm assuming that he's using Dr. Hanson. He's the best vocal cord surgeon in LA. Nate mentioned the appointment is first thing in the morning."

"How about where he's staying?"

"He usually gets a suite at the Four Seasons Beverly Hills when he's in LA. It's close to West Coast Records' offices."

"I know it well. Ivy stayed there while renovations were being done on her house."

"One more thing. Don't tell Nate you're coming. You know how he hates accepting help."

"I've got it covered. He'll never know what hit him."

"You're a doll," Melody said. "I've been sick, thinking about him all alone after the surgery."

"Don't worry," Mia said. "I'll take excellent care of him."

"I know you will. And he might never admit it, but I think he'll be really glad to have you there."

Three

The morning of his surgery Nate's thoughts were running on a hamster wheel, getting him nowhere. Not being able to talk for several weeks was going to make communicating with his clients a challenge. Although he'd asked for Mia's help from her father and sister, he hadn't approached her about acting as his voice for the next three to four weeks.

It wasn't that he couldn't hire an assistant with ASL experience, although it might be tricky finding one on such short notice. He also wasn't worried that the studio was booked solid and people were counting on him. He dreaded getting turned down by Mia again.

Pushing all that to the side, Nate left his suite and headed to the elevator. When the car arrived at his floor, a young couple with a baby stroller were already inside. Nate stepped to the side of the elevator and gazed from the infant to the happy parents. Almost against his will, his thoughts turned to Mia.

During those days with her on tour, for the first time ever, he'd contemplated what it would take to balance life on the road with a family. With the amount of touring Free Fall had done for the first few years when they were making a name for themselves, Nate hadn't even considered settling down.

Promoting an album meant grueling months on the road. It wasn't the sort of thing where you dragged a wife and kids along. Well, some people did. But unless it was the right sort of relationship, traveling from one end of the country to another put a lot of strain on a couple.

And then he'd met Mia. She was used to long months of touring and being away from home. As Ivy's personal assistant, she was on the go constantly. In fact, he wasn't entirely sure if she had a home of her own. He'd easily pictured them working together in the studio and then going out on tour. If they had a baby, the whole family would travel. It had been an appealing fantasy.

The elevator opened on the lobby and the couple with the stroller exited. Nate's mood, already battered by his anxiety about the surgery, took another hit. Damn, he was tired of being alone.

Suddenly every muscle in his body ached. He hadn't felt a sweeping depression like this in ten years. Back then he'd fought off the darkness with pills, booze and sex. None of it had helped, but for a while he'd been able to forget.

Nate stepped into the lobby, calling himself all kinds of coward and idiot for trying to handle things on his own. He was always the first one to lend a hand if someone needed it. Why did he have such an awful time accepting help?

Shame. Admitting that he wasn't strong enough to protect his mother when he was a kid or conquer an addiction to drugs when he was in his early twenties had led to both situations becoming worse. If he'd reached out for help, maybe his mom wouldn't have been nearly beaten to death by his father and he wouldn't have ended up burning bridges in the music business.

Nate headed across the hotel lobby and outside to where a car should be waiting to take him to the doctor's office. He'd turned down Trent's and Melody's offers to help, and he wasn't feeling great about his decision. But he hated being a bother. Trent was out of town with Savannah and Dylan. Melody was in Las Vegas. And while his mother would have happily flown in from Dallas to baby him for a few days, Nate didn't want to put her out. The surgery was delicate, but not overly invasive, and he was perfectly capable of taking care of himself.

And then the most amazing thing happened. A familiar brunette got up from a chair near the front door and started walking in his direction. Her appearance was so unexpected that he rubbed his eyes to determine if he was hallucinating. If so, she was the most beautiful, wonderful, perfect figment of his imagination he'd ever experienced.

"Mia?"

"At last," she said, gliding into step beside him. "I was worried that I'd missed you. How are you doing?" She peered up at him as the lobby doors opened with a whoosh and fresh air poured over them. "Are you nervous?"

"What are you doing here?"

"I'm here to take care of you." She gave him a stern look. "Why didn't you tell me you were having surgery?"

His first impulse was to tell her he didn't think it would matter to her. But that was a crappy response. He also hadn't thought she'd be available since her sister kept her so busy.

Instead he asked, "How did you know?"

"Melody told me. She said you didn't have anyone to help you after the surgery and she was worried." The look Mia shot him was pure accusation. "And so was I."

"I'll be perfectly fine."

"Ridiculous. A doctor won't release anyone going under anesthesia unless they're being picked up and watched over by a responsible adult. So, I'm going to sit in the waiting room while you have your surgery. And then I'm going to bring you back here. Tuck you in. And keep watch over you."

All that sounded like pure heaven. Having her fuss over him for the next few hours would speed his recovery along.

"You don't need to wait," he told her as they settled into the back of the town car. "The procedure could take up to six hours."

"I'm staying." Her tone was firm. "I brought stuff to read."

"Thank you." Such simple words didn't convey his full emotions. He was so damned glad to have her with him. But she smiled as if she understood.

Nate didn't feel much like talking on the way to the clinic, so they sat in companionable silence. The surgery was the most terrifying thing he'd ever faced and that included the night his sixteen-year-old self had gone up against his drunk, knife-wielding father.

Singing was more than just Nate's livelihood. It was how he'd comforted himself as a kid in an abusive home and the way he communicated who he was to the world.

No matter how successful he became as a producer and songwriter, he'd give up every penny he had to be able to perform on stage. This was something he hadn't realized until he was faced with the grim prospect of throat surgery.

When the nurse came to take him into the back, Mia gave him a reassuring smile. It was her face that filled his thoughts as he was wheeled to the operating room and injected with something to put him to sleep.

And when he woke what seemed like seconds later—in post-op, he guessed, based on the dim lighting and hushed silence—her name was the first thought that popped into his head. He floated in post-surgery haze, happy that she was waiting to take him back to his hotel As the residual anesthesia wore off, Nate lifted fingers to his throat, but the discomfort was all on the inside. Had the surgery been successful? He wouldn't know for several weeks, maybe months.

A nurse came to check on him and asked yes-or-no questions he could answer by nodding or shaking his head. She reiterated what the doctor and all the nurses before her had drilled into him: no talking of any kind for two to three weeks and minimal use of his voice after that. He'd start working with a vocal coach in a month, which would be a new experience. In all the years he'd performed, Nate had never had any formal training. He just got up on stage and let 'er rip.

They wanted him back in three days for a checkup, after which he could return to Las Vegas to continue healing. The nurse recommended Throat Coat tea with honey and gave him a prescription for pain meds.

"Your throat will probably grow more uncomfortable as the day goes on. Drink lots of fluids and remember, no talking."

Nate nodded. He might suck at taking advice on most things, but this he intended to follow to the letter. He couldn't imagine losing the ability to sing and perform. While he had songwriting and producing to fall back on, the energy that came at him from a packed stadium was a high he craved.

From post-op they sent him back into the waiting room, where Mia was still waiting, and gave him a glass of water. It slid down his throat without too much irritation and he grew hopeful.

"Are you okay?" Mia asked, giving his hand a gentle squeeze. "Let me know when you're ready to head to the car."

He nodded.

The trip back to the hotel was a blur. When they arrived at his suite, Nate fumbled out his key card and tried to focus on getting it into the slot. He wanted to curse, but knew better than to speak. And then, Mia plucked the key from him and within seconds the door swung open. He took a step forward and his head picked that second to swim. With his reflexes not quite back to normal, he swayed and made a grab for the doorframe just in time to prevent himself from pitching forward.

Her arm went around his waist to steady him. "I've got you," she said, but she wasn't as calm and collected as she sounded. Her brown eyes looked huge in her pale face.

"I'm okay, really."

She looked so appalled that he almost laughed, but he knew better than to make a sound.

"You okay?"

She gave a husky laugh. "I'll be better once you're in bed and resting."

"I knew you'd been dying to get me back into bed." His dry smile didn't help ease the tense line between her brows. And then, becoming more serious, he signed, *"It means a lot that you're here."*

He wanted to follow it up by asking how long she could stay, but again sensed the answer wouldn't make him happy. For now, he'd enjoy her company and take what time with her he could get.

"I'm sorry things between us didn't work out..." She was prevented from saying more by his fingertips against her lips.

He didn't want to talk about the failure of their relationship or argue about Mia's inability to escape her sister's demands. His arms ached to hold her. At the moment he didn't have energy to do more than sit on the couch with her snuggled against him, though.

"Come." He patted the cushion beside him.

"You should go to bed."

"I'm not tired."

For an instant he worried she might call him on that, but then she joined him on the couch.

"At least lie down."

He obliged by shifting until he lay on his back, his head in her lap. She ran her fingers through his hair. The soothing caress made his whole body ache. Damn, but he'd missed her. How many times in the last month had he relived those precious few hours they'd spent together that last night in Sydney? Over and over the memories tumbled through his mind as he recalled every touch and kiss. The ravenous hunger with which they'd come together that first time. The ache in his chest as the sun lifted above the horizon. The glorious, joyful goddess he'd held in his arms, who faded before his eyes as the morning grew brighter.

He'd sworn then that he would have her. All of her. He intended to do whatever it took to make her happy. Only she would have none of it. None of him. She didn't understand what it meant to be selfish. To demand happiness. Her family had molded her into someone who put her needs after everyone else's.

He closed his eyes and enjoyed the silence. With Mia he'd learned to appreciate being quiet, for it allowed him to be fully in the moment. Almost immediately, however, Nate found himself drifting off, and fought to stay awake. He'd learned during those long weeks on tour to savor every minute with Mia, because all too often their secret rendezvous were interrupted. But with what he'd gone through earlier today, his body craved sleep.

The next time he woke the suite was dim. His head remained cushioned on Mia's lap. He rubbed his face and sat up.

"What time is it?" he signed.

"Six. How are you feeling?"

"Sore."

"I'll get you some water." She got to her feet and headed for the wet bar consisting of a mini-fridge behind a white panel door. When she returned and handed him a chilled bottle, she asked, "Do you want to take something?"

He shook his head. Although the pain in his throat required medication to take the edge off, he didn't like the way the drugs made him feel. Early in his career he'd gotten caught up in the highs and lows of the music scene and had partied too hard. He'd relied on booze and pills to jack him up and mellow him out. And then there had always been girls. They were relentless. He'd signed boobs and butts. He'd taken two to bed and woken up with a third. And all this had happened before Free Fall had their first hit.

Then one morning, Nate had woken up with a thick head and a sick feeling in his gut that had nothing to do with how much he'd consumed the night before. There was a fist-size dent in his hotel room wall and a descriptive expletive written in lipstick on his bathroom mirror. He remembered being angry, but not why. It had been perfectly clear, however, that he'd struck out in anger. Just like his old man used to do.

Nate didn't have any luck tracking down the girl he'd brought back to his room. She'd just been one of the faceless hangers-on who liked to party after the concerts. He'd been twenty-three and the wake-up call had changed his life. He took a break from the band and returned home to Las Vegas, where he'd spent the next twelve months writing music.

It hadn't been an easy time. For the first two

months neither the words nor the music would flow. The urge to lose himself in alcohol or drugs had been a constant nagging presence. Much of the songwriting he'd done to that point had been while he was under the influence. He was afraid he didn't know how to write any other way. At that time his mom had still been living in Las Vegas. Being around her kept him from backsliding. He had only to look at her to remember how his father had gone after her with fists and eventually a knife.

At long last the music came more easily. The words took a lot longer. What he wanted to say came from his pain and his isolation and his sense of failure. These were not easy places to visit. He'd never really come to terms with the young boy who'd been too afraid to defend his mother. While a rational part of him knew it was ridiculous to expect a kid to take on a drunk, belligerent adult with a murderous temper, Nate knew there were things he should have done.

Like tell someone. His teacher. A cop. Anyone who could help. His mom had never learned to read lips and had had a hard time communicating. Nate became her voice from the time he could speak. But when it counted, he hadn't spoken for her.

"Are you hungry?" Mia asked. "I can heat up some soup. I brought you some of my famous chicken broth. And I have Throat Coat tea with honey."

Nate gazed up at her in bemusement. If this was what it felt like to be the beneficiary of Mia's nurturing, no wonder Ivy kept her sister on such a tight leash. How wonderful to have someone so focused on your every need.

I could get used to having you around all the time, he thought, but instead signed. *"I'm hungry."*

He hadn't noticed his empty stomach until Mia mentioned the soup. The thought of eating something she'd prepared with her lovely hands made him smile.

"What?" she asked, taking in his expression.

"I can't believe you're here."

"Well, don't get used to it," she teased, heading to the fridge once more. "You only get me for three days."

She busied herself pulling out a plastic container and ladling soup into a bowl. The suite had only the bare minimum of supplies—a coffeemaker, cups and a microwave, in addition to the small refrigerator—but somehow Mia presented a lovely tray with silverware, a linen napkin and even a tiny vase with a daisy in it.

"All this for me?" he signed as she placed the tray on his lap.

"Eat what you can. And there's vanilla and caramel gelato for dessert if you think you can manage it."

Instead of joining him on the couch, she sat in a chair nearby and watched him like a hawk as he tasted the soup. "Is it okay? Not too bland?"

"It's delicious."

"You should be able to switch to thicker liquids and soft foods tomorrow. Maybe some creamy cauliflower or broccoli soup?" He'd once told her he hated any sort of pureed vegetable, and wondered if she was taking perverse pleasure in his situation. When he scowled at her, she laughed. "Macaroni and cheese?"

"Better." And then, since he had her full attention, he added, *"It means a lot to me that you're here."*

Mia drew her knees to her chest, making herself as small as possible. He would have no idea how much his heartfelt words meant to her. Actually, it wasn't his words as much as the look in his eyes that warmed her from the tips of her fingers down to her toes. In the weeks they'd spent apart, she didn't remember ever feeling so alone and empty.

"We promised to be there for each other always," she reminded him, proud that she sounded so steady. He couldn't know what a struggle it was for her to keep from throwing herself into his arms and confessing how miserable she'd been without him. "What sort of friend would I be if I let you go through this alone?"

She knew Nate had trained himself to catch all sorts of subtle nuances in a singer's voice: pitch, strain, emotion. And he could do the same with her. While on tour, it had been pretty obvious that she'd been an open book to him. And he'd capitalized. If it had been another man, Mia might have worried that she was being manipulated into falling into bed. But Nate was a straight arrow. Not one person in the industry had anything but glowing comments about him, personally or professionally.

"We did promise." He gave her a lopsided smile. *"Which brings me to something I spoke to your father about last night. How would you feel about acting as my translator for the next month until I get my voice back?"*

How would she feel? Thrilled. Honored. Slightly terrified. Spending an extended amount of time with him, she was bound to let slip that she was massively crazy about him. Would she have the strength to stick by her original decision if once again he demanded she choose between him and her sister?

The way things were with Ivy at the moment, Mia couldn't leave her. But the opportunity to sit beside Nate while he worked his magic on Ivy's album was worth the risk.

"You talked to my father about this?"

"I wanted to make sure you couldn't use your sister as an excuse to turn me down."

Mia made a face at him. "And both Ivy and my dad were on board?"

"Your sister wasn't thrilled, but she understands in order to have me work on her album in a time frame that fits with her schedule, I'm going to need your special skills."

This arrangement seemed perfect. Ivy would get her album recorded. Mia could keep an eye on her and at the same time spend hours and hours with Nate. A month. It wasn't a lot of time, but it was more than she'd ever expected to have with him after they'd parted in Sydney.

"When do we start?"

"I'm heading back to Vegas on Tuesday after I check in with Dr. Hanson."

"I haven't had a chance to ask. How did your dinner with Ivy and my dad go last night?"

"Did you know your sister wants to record some of Melody's songs?"

"No." Ivy had been acting weird since the tour ended. She'd become more demanding than ever, driving Mia half mad with her quicksilver moods and indecision. And now this. "I guess I shouldn't be surprised. Melody is a talented songwriter and Ivy wants to work with the best."

"I tried to talk her out of it. What you composed during the tour was fantastic."

"She thinks my songs are what are preventing her from moving to the next level." Mia picked at a button on her blouse. "What if she's right? Maybe trying something new will get her that superstardom she craves."

"And what about you?"

"What about me?"

"Are you ready to take your career to the next level?"

"I don't think there's a level above personal assistant." Mia shot Nate a wry grin. But his question had merit.

What did she want to be doing ten years from now? The thought of continuing to cater to her sister's every whim made her stomach churn. Mia supposed their father wouldn't want to manage Ivy forever. Mia could step into that role. Did she want to? If she was honest with herself, she'd admit that more than anything else she wanted to write music.

"I was thinking more in terms of songwriting."

"It's not the easiest way to make a living."

"You might need to combine it with something else to support yourself. Like producing."

"Do you know how many female producers there are in the industry?"

Nate shook his head.

"Neither does anyone else," Mia said with a touch of reproach. "Because the number is so small no one bothers to keep track. But it's around 5 percent."

"How do you know that?"

"When *1989* won the Grammy for album of the year, Taylor Swift talked in her acceptance speech about empowering women and how we should take credit for our own success."

Mia had been sitting alone in Ivy's house, watching the show and feeling a little sick to her stomach at how she hadn't fought for songwriting credit on either of her twin's albums.

"Afterward," Mia continued, "she was criticized for how few women she'd had working on her album.

Nineteen people, excluding Taylor, worked on *1989*. Of those, only two were women. That means 11 percent of the production team were female. That's double the percentage of women in the industry."

"Women are underrepresented. How do you feel about changing that? Do you want to?"

"I won't lie and say I've never thought about it. I've been creating beats since Ivy recorded her first single. I know what I would have done to make the song better. Although I've sat in on every one of Ivy's studio sessions, most of what I know about the technical side is from watching other people."

"Is that a yes or no?"

"That's a hell yes, for spending several weeks sitting beside you and learning the ins and outs of what makes you such a fantastic producer. Beyond that I can't say what will happen."

Nate gave a satisfied nod and didn't try to push for anything more. Mia was glad for both their sakes. He'd been so frustrated with her that last morning in Sydney when she dug in her heels and refused to even consider taking time off from her sister and spending it with him. She hadn't seen the point in furthering their relationship when it was all bound to come to an end.

She might have given him a different answer if Nate had been the sort of guy who wanted something casual and would be happy to walk away at any point. If she could've sneaked away here and there for a long weekend with him they might still be involved.

But that wasn't the sort of guy he was. At least not with her. He'd been pretty clear from the start that she was special to him. While he hadn't minded keeping their blossoming romance a secret during the tour, everything had changed after they'd made love. He'd wanted to see her openly and as often as possible.

Ivy would freak if she ever found out Mia and Nate were involved. Especially now that she had some crazy idea that she and Nate were destined for each other. Mia wasn't ready for the upheaval it would cause for her family.

"How's your throat?" She cleared away his tray and brought him some gelato.

"It's great."

But she could tell from the tension in his facial muscles that wasn't true. "Where are your pain meds?"

"I don't want to take them."

Mia was torn. As much as she hated seeing him endure the pain, she had selfish reasons for being glad he'd refused to take the drugs. "Let me get you some water. Everything I've read advises staying hydrated."

She handed him a full water bottle and he signed his thanks. For no good reason, Mia's eyes prickled with sudden tears. Damn this man for turning her into a sappy mess with a simple thank-you. Not trusting her voice, and since saying "you're welcome" wasn't done in American Sign Language, she responded by signing *"no problem"* before turning away.

Despite his short nap earlier, Nate seemed tired, so after watching television together for an hour, she shooed him toward the bedroom. He caught her hand and, before she knew what he intended, dropped a kiss in her palm.

"Are you going to stay?" he signed, his lips curved into a hopeful smile.

The entreaty in his gray eyes messed with her pulse. She'd come prepared to spend the night, but hadn't intended on forcing her presence on him.

"I can."

He wrapped his arm around her waist and drew her against his solid body. Lean muscle shifted beneath her fingertips as she put her hand on his upper abdomen to keep a little space between them.

"On the couch," she added with a shaky laugh.

He shook his head and then tipped it to the side and put his free hand against his cheek to sign *"bed."* Her toes curled at the thought of lying beside him while he slept, listening to his even breathing, tormented by his powerful frame mere inches away. If they shared a bed there was no way she was going to get any sleep tonight.

Every time she shut her eyes she relived that night in Sydney. Sneaking kisses in out-of-the-way places during the early stages of their secret tour romance had been wildly exciting, but nothing had prepared her for the intensity of his mouth on her breasts or the surprising way his muscles shivered beneath her questing fingers.

The memory of making love with him hadn't grown the least bit fuzzy with each week that passed. Nor had her feelings for him dulled. For the last month and a half she'd thrown herself into everything that could take her mind off Nate for even a fraction of a second. Sticking close to Ivy made this pretty easy. And late at night Mia wrote music. Heartbreaking songs of love and loss that belonged on a country music album. They weren't the pop styling of Ivy Bliss.

"Go to bed. I'll be in after I call Melody and let her know you're okay. I sent her a text while you napped earlier, but she'll want some details."

He kissed the top of her head and stepped back. *"Don't be long."*

"Tyrant."

"This is nothing. Wait until you see me in the control booth."

Mia called Melody and gave her an update on how Nate was doing, and shared that she'd be translating for him for the next month so he could keep his production schedule.

"What a great idea. I know Nate signs because his mother is deaf. How did you learn?"

"My older sister, Eva, lost her hearing when she was two." While Mia and her mother were fluent,

Ivy and their father never learned to sign beyond some basic words.

"You haven't talked about her much. Does she live in California?"

"Chicago. She's a psychiatrist and a lot of her patients are hearing impaired." Talking about Eva made sadness swell inside Mia. With her sister so far away and both of them so busy, she didn't get a chance to see her as often as she'd like.

"How did Nate know you could sign?" Melody jumped in and answered her own question before Mia could say a word. "That's how you two communicated when Ivy was around."

Heat crept into Mia's cheeks. "Sometimes."

"I never did understand why you and Nate were so determined to keep your relationship a secret."

"Things like that get complicated around my sister."

"I mean that crush she had on him was, like, seven years ago. And it's not as if he encouraged her. Nate said he deleted every one of her texts."

"Wait…" Mia shook her head and tried to assimilate what Melody was saying. "Ivy had a crush on Nate?" Why hadn't he ever mentioned this to her?

"I thought you were glued to her every second of every day."

Mia rolled her eyes. "Now I am. Seven years ago I was finishing high school, like every other normal eighteen-year-old, while my twin sister was singing and acting on Broadway." That had been around the time when Mia's life stopped being normal. "Tell me what happened?"

"Apparently she got ahold of his phone number and sent him a bunch of texts, telling him how much she loved his music and begging him to come visit her in New York. Didn't Nate tell you?"

"No." Why not? Was that why Ivy had gotten so excited about the prospect of working with Nate? Because she'd had a crush on him a long time ago? "Did he go to New York?"

"Ohmygod, no. He wasn't interested. She isn't his type. He said he had to talk to your dad before it stopped."

Was this a contributing factor to why Mia had had to rush to New York and take a GED exam instead of graduating with her class?

"You should ask Nate about it," Melody continued.

"I will. And speaking of Ivy, Nate said she wants to record some of your songs." Mia was relieved no grief sounded in her tone. Although she was sad and disappointed that Ivy no longer wanted to record her songs, the fact that Ivy and their father had made the decision and not bothered to tell her was what really hurt.

"Which ones?"

"I have no idea."

"I guess I'd better decide which songs I want for my album or Ivy will snap up all my best stuff."

Melody laughed, but there wasn't much humor in it. "Tell Nate I'm thinking about him."

"Will do."

After Mia hung up, she picked up her overnight bag and headed into the bedroom. Nate was propped up on the pillows, his eyes alert and intense. Mia tried to keep her gaze from lingering on his bare torso, but his broad shoulders and muscular arms awakened her hormones and stirred up her desires. His lower half was hidden by the sheet and she prayed that he was wearing pajama bottoms.

"I'm going to change," she murmured awkwardly, heading into the bathroom.

"I've seen—" he began signing, but she was through the door before he could finish. One nice thing about his inability to speak was that all she had to do to get in the last word was not look at him.

She took her time changing into pajamas. She wasn't primping, but hoping that he might fall asleep while waiting for her.

He hadn't. And as she stepped into the bedroom and saw the glint in his eye, she wondered if either of them would feel rested come morning.

Four

"*Sexy,*" Nate signed, grinning as Mia's expression contorted into chagrin.

She dodged his mocking smile and glanced down at her bright blue sleepwear. "What did you expect?"

If she thought covering herself from chin to ankle was going to distract him from her luscious body, she'd underestimated her appeal. Then he sighed. Isn't that what she always did? Undervalued her worth.

"Something see-through and short."

"Ha. I didn't ask what you wanted." She set her bag on the chair next to the window and circled the bed like a wary alley cat confronted by a rival tom. "You're here to recover and I'm here to make sure you get lots of rest."

"Boring."

"I suggest you appreciate the peace and quiet. You're going to have my sister in your recording studio for the next month."

"Come here." He motioned her closer. *"I don't want to talk about your sister."*

Mia crossed her arms over her chest and shook her head. "Why didn't you tell me Ivy had a thing for you seven years ago?"

If Nate could've made a noise, what would've come out of him was a groan. *"Because it was seven years ago. And no big deal."*

"You rejected my sister. Do you seriously think she lets things like that go? She's still mad because Jimmy Reynolds picked me to be his buddy the day we went to the zoo in second grade."

Nate had little trouble believing Ivy couldn't let things go, but surely Mia was exaggerating about her sister holding a grudge because of a second-grade field trip.

Mia threw up her hands. "No wonder she was so cool to you on tour."

Had Ivy been cool? He must've looked puzzled because Mia asked, "You didn't notice the way she flirted with everyone except you?"

He shook his head. In fact he hadn't noticed much about Ivy at all. His attention had all been focused on Mia.

"It explains a lot," she said. "And now she thinks

because you want to work with her that you're interested."

Nate wasn't particularly worried. He was a professional and would treat her as such. *"I'm only interested in you."*

Mia's color was high as she approached the bed. "You can't be interested in me. We've been through this already."

"And it didn't end the way I wanted to." He paused to read her expression. *"I don't think it ended the way you wanted, either."*

"What I want hasn't mattered since I was seventeen years old."

"Why?"

She waved her hand, batting his question away. "It's a complicated family thing. Ivy isn't as strong as she appears. She needs me to be there for her."

For how long? The rest of her life? Mia had so much to offer. If only she'd stop hiding behind her sister.

"When you say she needs you to be there for her," Nate began, bringing up something he should've probably saved for another time. *"Does that include making excuses for her when she doesn't feel like doing something?"*

To his mind, Ivy could stand to concern herself with something more than her immediate needs and desires. Maybe she'd grow up a little if she took some responsibility. He wasn't sure that Mia was doing her sister any favors by shielding her.

Mia pressed her lips together and held still for a long moment before offering up a long sigh. "Yes."

He made a rude gesture.

As always Mia was quick to make excuses for her sister. "She's an artist and artists are sensitive."

Nate wanted to point out that he was an artist, as well, and that didn't stop him from dragging his ass out of bed when he was exhausted or showing up on time and ready to work even when he didn't feel like writing or singing or being interviewed.

"That's not going to cut it in my studio. My time is money."

Mia's resistance crumbled. "I know. I'll warn her about that."

"Come here."

This time she didn't resist. Once he had her beneath the covers, he slid down until he lay flat on his back. The urge to reach across the foot of space separating them on the mattress and touch her overpowered him, but she shook her head, as if she could read his intentions.

"We can't."

"You want to."

"Yes," she whispered, even as she shook her head. "But I can't." And then she turned onto her side and put her back to him with a mumbled good-night.

He signed his response, knowing she couldn't see it, and rolled onto his side away from her before temptation had him rolling her onto her back and covering her mouth with his. Not that he had the energy to make love to her. Damn it all. It figured that he'd get her back into bed when he couldn't capitalize on it. On the other hand, she wouldn't be here at all if not for his surgery.

Nate drifted off to sleep, keenly aware that bare inches separated his back from Mia's. However, at some point during the night, they both shifted, and when he woke up she was nestled beside him, her softness warming his left side, her cheek pillowed on his chest. His arm was around her. He'd buried his nose in her sweetly fragrant hair.

From her deep, even breathing he decided she was still asleep, so he kept perfectly still and savored the moment. Outside, the sun was kissing the balcony railing. Nate closed his eyes and pretended that he still had hours and hours to enjoy having his arms around Mia.

He guessed it was no more than twenty minutes later when she woke. Her body tensed as she became aware of their position, and almost immediately she began to disentangle herself. He tightened his fingers.

"How long have you been awake?" she asked, resisting his hold for several seconds before her muscles went limp once more.

He signed *"twenty minutes"* with his right hand and then placed his fingers beneath her chin to shift her head back. Their eyes met as he lowered his lips to hers.

She sighed into his mouth and he deepened the

kiss, tracing her lips and teeth with his tongue until she let him in. His heart ached as her fingers stroked his cheek before latching on to his hair to pull him closer. She groaned against his mouth. Her morning kisses were sweet, with just a hint of sexy. Since he couldn't tell her how amazing she tasted or how soft her lips were, he did his best to let her know with his fingers against her cheek and neck.

"I don't think this is what the doctor ordered," she half moaned as he worked his lips down her throat. With a breathless laugh, she ducked away from the hand he'd slipped beneath the hem of her pajama top and half rolled, half shimmied off the bed.

"I was told not to speak. He said nothing about sex."

"I'm sure you were told not to exert yourself."

Her color was already high and his wicked grin drove the brightness in her cheeks even higher. She caught her lip between her teeth and stared at his bare chest for a long moment before shaking her head.

"I'm going to make you some Throat Coat tea and order you a smoothie for breakfast."

Nate watched her go before rolling out of bed and heading into the bathroom for a shower. When he came out, a bottle of water awaited him on the countertop by the sink. Mia was serious about keeping him hydrated. He dressed and headed into the living room, wondering how he was going to keep himself occupied and his hands off Mia for the next couple days. Idleness wasn't something he did well. If he wasn't working in the studio, he was writing music or promoting the band.

"I don't suppose you want to share what you've been working on lately with me?" he signed after breakfast.

"I have a couple beats I recorded the other day. When Ivy decided she wanted to change things up a bit, I started playing with some synthpop sounds." Mia frowned slightly. "Of course, that was before I learned she wants to record Melody's music."

"Let me hear."

She pulled out her phone and scanned through until she found the track she was looking for. When she played it for him, his eyes widened. It was very different from anything Ivy had done. Perhaps a little too different for the pop princess?

"Has Ivy heard this?"

"I can read your mind," Mia said with a self-conscious sigh. "I know it's different from her usual stuff. And no, I haven't played any of this for her."

"I know a couple singers who might be interested in what you have there." Nate paused and gave her a second to digest that. *"I can give them a call. Or send them a text,"* he amended.

"I'll think about it. It's all pretty rough at the moment."

"Maybe when we get into the studio you can play around with it some more."

"Maybe." She gave a noncommittal shrug. "By

the way, I mentioned to Melody that Ivy is interested in recording some of her music, so she can prepare."

"I'm sure she appreciated the heads-up."

Mia's phone buzzed and she glanced at the screen. From her grimace, Nate assumed it was her sister calling. She got up and took the phone out to the small terrace.

"Hi, Ivy, what's up?" Mia stood with her back to him, but it didn't prevent her voice from carrying back into the suite. There was a pause, during which she paced from one end of the terrace to the other. "I can't, because I'm out of town. I drove up the coast for a couple days."

She turned in Nate's direction so he signed at her.

"Liar."

"Shut up." And then she sat on one of the chairs and leaned her forehead on her hand. "Dad hasn't talked to me about the direction for your new album."

Nate wondered what it would take for Mia to come clean about their relationship. What was the harm in explaining that she'd spent last night helping him out after his surgery? The dynamic between the sisters continued to baffle him.

"Of course I understand that you want to work with Melody Caldwell. She's incredibly talented." A long pause, then, "No, I'm not upset. I just needed a break…from LA. Can we talk about this later?"

When Mia hung up with her sister, she blew out a big breath.

"What did she want?"

"For me to run some errands."

"Your talents are wasted on your sister."

"It's more complicated than that." But she didn't defend her situation as adamantly as she'd done in the past. "She really does need me."

Not wishing to spoil their limited time together with an argument, Nate held out his hand and gestured Mia toward him. There would be plenty of time in the next month for them to discuss her future and for him to convince her to leave her sister and stay with him.

"Come play more of what you've been working on."

A week after Nate's surgery, Mia found herself in the lobby of Ugly Trout Records with her sister and father. The spare, utilitarian space was like Nate. Unpretentious and purposeful. There was a beige leather sectional beneath the company logo rendered in copper on the wall. On the opposite wall six guitars hung in a neat line. It wasn't designed to impress executives or big name stars. Musicians came to Las Vegas to record and work with Nate. His stellar reputation was all the promotion the label required.

Mia followed Ivy and their father through the glass door that led from the lobby into the empty conference room. They were late and Mia grimaced, wondering how upset Nate was at the moment.

"I'm surprised he isn't here to greet us," Ivy said,

pulling a small mirror out of her purse to check her appearance yet again.

"Me, too, especially since we're fifteen minutes late."

Ivy shot her a dirty look. "What's gotten into you all of a sudden?"

Mia bit the inside of her cheek and reminded herself that this session would not go well if Ivy was upset. "It's just that I promised Nate we would be here right at ten." The second she used "we" Mia knew she'd screwed up.

"He's expecting *me*."

"Of course." Mia used her most soothing tone. "But you need me to translate what he's saying."

Ivy went back to checking her appearance. "If you think this makes you special, it doesn't. Remember that it's me he asked to work with."

Because he wants to spend time with me. But Mia didn't dare speak the truth out loud. Ivy wouldn't believe her. She barely believed it herself. Why was someone as talented and successful as Nate Tucker interested in a nobody like her?

A couple minutes later Nate, Melody and two men entered the room. The very air seemed to change with Nate's presence and Mia's eyes were glued to him as he came around the conference table to shake hands with Ivy. The rest of his team followed suit. When all the introductions had been made, Nate's gaze sought Mia.

He raised an eyebrow before signing. *"Let's get started, shall we?"*

Mia translated, and for a while the only sound in the room was her voice as she followed Nate's hands. He spoke about Ivy's previous two albums with West Coast Records and how the songs had been great, but the production had been rushed on both.

When Ivy had originally been signed by the label, the company had been run by Siggy Caldwell, Trent and Melody's father. In the past month, Nate and Trent had purchased the failing record company and planned to restore it to its former glory.

"We're going to develop a better marketing strategy for releasing her music this time," Nate signed.

"I'm glad to hear that," Javier Navarro said. "The delays in releasing her last album really hurt the sales."

"Trent and I agree."

"I've been dying to work with you and Melody," Ivy said. "When can I get into the studio?"

Nate glanced toward Melody. *"Studio C is open right now. Why don't you two run through a few songs. I want to give Mia a tour and introduce her to some people she'll be working with this next month."*

Ivy's eyes narrowed. "I thought she was going to translate for you."

"She is."

"Then why does she need a tour?"

"Your sister showed an interest in sound production and she's going to need to learn what I'm talk-

ing about in order to make people understand what I'm asking for."

"Whatever."

When Melody led Ivy and Javier out of the conference room, Mia turned to Nate. A blend of resignation and anxiety caused her chest to tighten. Conscious of the production assistants that remained in the room, Mia signed, *"You and I working together is going to make her crazy."*

"I don't care."

"I do. And you're not the one who has to live with her."

"You don't have to, either."

"Please tell me we're not going to have this discussion every day for the next month."

"It's not my fault that your sister misunderstands our relationship."

"By 'our relationship' do you mean yours and mine or yours and hers?"

"Both." Nate's eyes were liquid silver as his gaze settled on her lips. *"Now let's go find an empty studio so I can kiss you."*

"You are nothing but trouble," she declared.

The next four weeks were going to be heaven and hell. As much as it delighted her to be working so closely with Nate, keeping him at arm's length was going to be a nearly impossible task.

"When it comes to you I am very determined." He put his palm on her back and nudged her toward the door.

Just that fleeting touch sent her pulse skyrocketing. A nagging twinge in her chest bloomed into a sharp dig, but she smiled through it. Three days ago she'd woken in his arms and for a few minutes her world had been perfect. But the reality was that they couldn't be together. He wanted something that was impossible for her to give right at this moment. And she couldn't bring herself to hope that he'd wait around long enough for Mia to be reassured that her sister was strong enough to go it alone.

Mia's hands shook as Nate escorted her into a control room. She was relieved to find it occupied. On the other side of the glass, a group of studio musicians were jamming. The intensity of their concentration broke as the song came to an end. Smiles and high fives were shared all around.

Nate signed and then pushed a button. Mia stared at him until he made a gesture and she realized he wanted her to speak.

"Sounds good. This is Mia," she translated, then waved. "She's going to be my voice for the next month."

"You should keep her on permanently," a bald, barrel-chested guy with a goatee called out. "She sounds way better than you ever did."

"Looks a lot better, too."

Once the sound engineers introduced themselves, Nate indicated the door across the hall, which led to another control booth. In the studio a young man rapped to an intricate beat that Mia recognized as something Nate had been fooling around with during the tour.

"You wrote that."

He nodded before introducing her to the guy manning the booth. His name was Craig.

"*Moving on.*"

Nate opened the door to another studio and gestured her inside. The control booth on the other side of the glass was empty. The studio held a set of drums, a couple keyboards and several guitars.

As expected, he spun her around and pinned her against the door. He'd promised to find them an empty studio where he could kiss her, and he'd delivered. She didn't resist as his lips found hers and he stole her breath away. Damn. The man knew how to kiss. His tongue traced her lips until she parted for him. She expected him to deepen the kiss, and when he continued nipping and nibbling her lips, she was the one who pushed up onto her toes and took the kiss to the next level.

Both of them were breathing hard and flushed when he stepped back and signed.

"*Feel like fooling around?*"

"Depends…" She tucked the hem of her shirt back into her pants and drew the word out, wondering what Nate had in mind.

"*Give me a taste of what you've been working on. Just play around a bit with some of it and see what happens.*"

"I can play some of the melodies." Mia glanced at the instruments.

"And the lyrics."

This wasn't what she was accustomed to. Usually she recorded all her demos using her laptop, alone in her room with a keyboard, synthesizer and a guitar. She was free to make mistakes, and stop and start if things didn't work. She often danced around, as if that somehow could make the creative juices flow.

Nate was watching her closely. *"Okay?"*

She gave a reluctant nod. While on tour, Mia had written several songs inspired by her growing feelings for Nate.

She sat down at the keyboard, but with Nate watching, her mind was blank.

"Can you maybe go sit over there?" She indicated a stool behind her. "You're making me nervous."

"Why? You've played your songs for me before."

"That was messing around. This is your studio and you've kinda put me on the spot."

"Fine."

With him out of her line of sight, the music came rushing back. Mia set her fingers on the keys and played a chord. The notes filled the space, a comfortable cushion for her emotions. She stopped worrying what Nate might think and just set her songs free.

They were two ballads. Some of her best work. Not only had her romance with Nate infused her lyrics with deeper emotion, his musical genius had encouraged her to innovate. To say she was proud of them was an understatement.

But the songs were too personal. Mia had been speaking the truth of her heart. And as she finished playing, she realized she'd written them for Nate. Suddenly, she was very glad Ivy wouldn't record them. To hear her sister sing those lyrics before Mia had even come to terms with what they meant to her would have been awful.

As she turned to face Nate, she found herself holding her breath. His thoughtful expression gave her no clue to his opinion. At last she couldn't take it anymore. "Well?"

"I'd like to run both of those past the guys. Free Fall might be interested in recording one or both."

Mia couldn't stop the tears that flooded her eyes. It was the nicest thing he could've said to her. Nate got to his feet and took several steps in her direction, but she waved him off.

"I'm fine."

"I can't guarantee anything."

"I know." She gave a shaky laugh and wiped moisture away from the corners of her eyes. "It's just such a thrill that you'd even consider…" She trailed off and regarded him suspiciously. "This isn't a bribe to get me to sleep with you, is it?"

His mouth popped open, but he caught himself just in time and signed instead. *"If only I was that devious."* He headed for the door and motioned her out.

The last studio they entered was occupied by Melody and Ivy.

"How's it going?" Mia translated for Nate.

"She likes this one." Melody cued a demo. As her voice poured from the speakers, Melody caught Mia's gaze and gave her head the smallest of shakes.

"I thought you were looking to take your next album in a new direction," Nate signed. *"That's similar to what you did on your last two albums."*

"I don't want to be too different. The fans have certain expectations."

"What about 'Love Me More'?"

Melody cued another song and Mia immediately saw where Nate was going with his suggestion.

An unhappy line formed between Ivy's brows as the chorus started. Mia recognized the warning signs and glanced toward their father, but his expression was thoughtful.

"You'd kill this," Melody agreed.

The song would take Ivy in a whole new direction. It was less sexually charged, more empowered and upbeat. Her sister had mad dance skills and enjoyed moving around the stage. Recording music like this would demonstrate that Ivy could do more than just pout and smolder as she sang.

Unfortunately, Ivy was comfortable pouting and smoldering, and as much as she claimed she wanted to grow as an artist, she retreated back into the same old tricks, where she felt safe.

"Let's give it a try," Mia translated for Nate.

"Now?" Ivy's eyes widened. She hadn't come prepared to record anything. Usually she took weeks and weeks to rehearse a song before she entered the studio. Not only was she a perfectionist, she hated looking foolish.

"Let's see what we can do."

"I don't know the song."

"We'll take it slow."

When Mia repeated what Nate had signed, Ivy shot daggers at her. Mia recognized that Ivy wanted her to speak up on her behalf, but a thousand trifling slights and mistreatments held Mia's tongue. Ivy had claimed Mia's songs as her own on the last two albums and now she wanted a new sound. This was it. Mia glanced between her father and Nate while the tension built in the room.

Finally, after seeing that everyone expected her to agree, Ivy nodded reluctantly. "I'll give it a try."

"Wonderful."

Melody handed her the sheet music and Ivy shot Mia one last scowl before leaving the control booth for the recording studio. When Ivy stood in front of the mike, Nate cued a track and let the music play. Ivy listened for a while and then began to sing. Her vocals were soft and sexy like what she was used to performing and not at all what Nate was looking for.

He signed and cued the mike.

With a silent groan, Mia translated. "Don't be afraid to let go. This is a girl telling a boy to really love her. Get in his face about it."

Nate's eyes were on her as she finished speaking. One corner of his mouth twitched as their eyes met.

Ivy started again. Mia could tell her sister was tense and uncomfortable. At the halfway point of the song she quit. "This isn't working."

"I'm the producer. Why don't you let me judge what is and isn't going to work. Just sing," Nate signed. Mia translated, painful reluctance in her voice.

She was going to pay for this later.

Five

Nate almost felt sorry for Mia as she told her sister what he wanted. He understood the dynamic between them well enough to know that Mia was miserable relaying his suggestions for Ivy's performance. And Ivy was equally unhappy to receive them. But it had to be good for Mia to be the one in command for a change, even if only by proxy.

And in truth, as the hour went on, Mia's manner grew more confident and Ivy's interpretation of Melody's song evolved into what the songwriter had intended. It wasn't perfect, but it was a start.

"That's much better," Mia translated. "Why don't you come in here and listen to the playback."

"How did it feel to boss your sister around?"

"I wasn't. All I did was tell her what you said."

"Not word for word."

Mia rolled her eyes. *"Did you want her to storm out or keep singing?"*

"What are you two talking about?" Javier asked, breaking into their silent conversation.

"Sorry." Mia shot her father a rueful look. "I'm use to signing with Eva and I forgot that Nate can hear."

"Nice save."

"Nate was just saying how happy he is to be working with such a talented singer." Mia smiled in a way that dared Nate to argue.

As if he could. For all she caved to her sister's domineering ways, Mia had spunk and backbone. During the next four weeks, Nate intended to figure out why she let Ivy push her around, and to do whatever it took to steal her away.

"I enjoyed kissing you earlier."

Ivy entered the booth and sat beside her father on the couch.

"I enjoyed your singing." Obviously rattled, Mia blurted out the awkward translation. She pointed at Nate. "That's what he said."

"That's not what I said. By the way, you're blushing. How long do you think you can keep our relationship a secret?"

"Stop it," she signed back. *"And what relationship?"*

"The one where I tear your clothes off every chance I get."

Although he wanted to stare at Mia and see how

his declaration affected her, Nate nodded to the sound engineer, who queued the playback. Beside him, Mia radiated heat, but without glancing at her expression, he didn't know if she was struggling with annoyance or lust.

Ivy's voice filled the space. She'd sung along with a simple piano track that Melody had recorded for the demo. Nate heard the potential in what Ivy could do with the song and the hairs on the back of his neck rose in reaction. It was a good sign. Whether she believed it or not, the music suited her voice. The question remained whether she could get behind the words and sell it.

A collective sigh filled the control booth when the last notes tapered off. Nate nodded in satisfaction and pinned Ivy with his gaze. The woman was ridiculously talented. Pity she was such a diva.

Javier looked pleased with what he'd heard. "I think that's a keeper."

"I'd like to record the other song we discussed earlier, as well," Ivy said, obviously not willing to concede quite yet.

Nate wasn't about to negotiate with the pop princess. He looked at Melody. *"Give her the music for those five songs we talked about."* When Mia translated what he'd said, he turned to Ivy.

"Take the rest of the week and get a feel for the songs. I want you back in the studio on Friday. We'll work on all of them."

"You're only giving me three days. That's not

enough time," the pop princess squeaked, shooting a panicked look toward her father.

Javier shrugged. "If we want to get the album done in a short amount of time, you're going to have to commit to working hard."

Nate could almost hear Ivy's thoughts. She didn't want to work hard. She wanted to shop and party and boss her sister around.

Nate began signing again. "You have three days to learn five songs. They don't have to be perfect," Mia translated. "But you do need to have a feel for them."

"Fine." Ivy tossed her head and made her way to the door.

Before Mia could follow on her sister's heels, Nate caught her by the arm, stopping her. *"Want to be my date to the AMAs?"*

Free Fall had once again been nominated for favorite pop/rock duo or group, an award they'd won two years earlier, and favorite pop/rock album. The competition was especially stiff this year and he didn't expect they'd win. Having Mia sitting beside him would take the sting out of the loss.

"The AMAs?" Mia breathed, beaming at his invitation.

Ivy had reached the hall, but when she heard her sister speak, she whirled around. "What about the AMAs?"

Mia's delight dimmed. "Nate asked me to go with him."

"Why? To translate?"

Nate could tell she was about to lie to her sister once again. He caught her hand to get her attention and shook his head in warning. *"Tell her the truth."*

"As his date."

"Your date?" Ivy looked scandalized as she fixed Nate with her stare. "That's not possible."

"Why not?" Mia translated for him.

The pop star set her hand on her hip and thrust out her lower lip like a toddler. "Because she's my assistant."

And he was sick of the way Ivy treated Mia. *"She's also your sister,"* he signed, but Mia didn't immediately translate.

Both Nate and Ivy glared at her as she stood frozen in mute silence, gazing from one to the other. She deserved so much better than to be at Ivy's beck and call. What was wrong with the entire family that everything revolved around Ivy and her damned career?

"That means she'll already be there," Mia said at last, playing diplomat and not translating his exact words.

The last bit of Nate's patience was draining away. *"Don't let her bully you."*

"But it's Mia," Ivy stated, as if that would convince Nate to change his mind.

He nodded.

Mia finally found her own voice. "I'd love to go."

She spoke softly, but her eyes glowed. In moments like these she was more beautiful than her twin.

"But I need her backstage. I'm performing and presenting."

"You'll have Yvonne to help with your changes and makeup," Mia said. Now that she'd accepted his invitation, she appeared unwilling to back down. It was a nice change from the way she normally catered to her sister's every whim.

"She doesn't own anything that she can wear to an award show," Ivy said to Nate. Clearly, she wasn't giving up.

As a featured artist, Ivy would have her choice of gowns sent over by designers eager for the publicity. Mia didn't have that sort of celebrity and Nate doubted she had the pull to arrange her own red carpet gown.

"I have a stylist in LA who can hook you up," Nate signed. *"I'll give her a call."* He sighed. *"Send her a email."*

"That would be great," Mia breathed, without bothering to translate.

Her reverent expression left Nate wondering how often anything good came her way. It spurred him to work even harder to make the entire event something Mia would want more of. She'd spent far too much time being invisible, not thinking she deserved her moment in the sun. Getting her used to being treated like a celebrity was a step forward in his plan to wrestle her away from her sister.

"I'll make the arrangements. Don't let her talk you out of going with me."

"I won't." And then to Ivy she said, "We'd better head out if you want to make your massage appointment." And as her sister stormed away down the hall, Mia gave Nate one last glance and signed, *"Thank you."*

Mia carried the cup of Throat Coat tea into Ivy's bedroom. Their father had rented a five-bedroom house with a pool in a gated community for the month Ivy would be recording at Ugly Trout. It had been a week since meeting with Nate at the studio and whatever progress her sister was making with Melody's songs was negated by the fact that when Ivy wasn't at the studio, she was either out shopping or partying with her friends Skylar and Riley, who'd shown up from LA.

The appearance of those two raised Mia's concern. The party girls, whose only source of income was their sketchy modeling careers and fashion blog, weren't good for Ivy, who was far too prone to be distracted from what she'd come to Las Vegas to do. Mia had convinced their father to chase them out of the house early that morning so Ivy could work on the songs Nate wanted her to record, but from the pile of high-end shopping bags on the floor at the foot of Ivy's bed, he hadn't persuaded them to leave town.

The fact that her sister wasn't trying on her latest purchases or even admiring what she'd bought told Mia something was wrong. The curtains were drawn over the sliding glass door that led out to the pool.

It took a second for Mia to spot her twin. Ivy had pressed herself into a corner of the room, her knees tucked against her chest like a small child trying to make herself invisible. Tears streamed down her face and Mia's heart crashed to her toes.

"What's the matter?" She set the teacup on the bureau and went to sit before her sister. "I brought you some tea. Why don't you try to drink some."

Ivy stared right through her. "I can't do it. Nothing feels right. They're all expecting me to do something amazing and none of it is me." Ivy blinked and her eyes gained focus. She met Mia's gaze. "When we were on tour, I heard the songs Melody was working on and they sounded so wonderful. I want wonderful, but it's not happening."

"That's not true. I've been there, listening to you record. Everything you do is wonderful," Mia assured her sister, speaking from the heart. So often lately when she complimented Ivy it was because her sister expected the praise. But when Ivy was like this, when her demons crowded in, it was easy for Mia to give her twin every bit of support she had in her.

"Dad's expecting me to go platinum with this album, so it has to be perfect."

Mia had always thought having their father manage Ivy's career added extra pressure for her to succeed. In the same vein, if it hadn't been Daddy calling the shots, Ivy's image might be different. Mia was pretty sure her twin never would've had plastic surgery at seventeen and probably wouldn't have become addicted to the painkillers that almost killed her.

"Don't worry about Dad or Mom or what anyone else thinks."

No matter how well Ivy did, she always wanted to do better. And when she wasn't recognized, which was what had happened with this year's American Music Award nominations, things went downhill fast.

Since mid-October, when the nominations were announced and Ivy's name hadn't appeared anywhere, Mia had been scrambling harder than ever to keep her sister happy. As ambitious as she was beautiful and talented, Ivy had grown positively obsessed with making her next album grittier, sexier, more over-the-top than anything she'd done so far.

Mia thought her sister was on the wrong track. It was why Ivy and Nate were butting heads. If Ivy wanted to be taken seriously as an artist, she needed to become more authentic rather than a caricature of the personality she'd become.

"Make music that's in your heart," Mia continued. "Let it speak to who you are."

Ivy's lips curved into a sad smile. "What if I don't know who that is?"

"You'll figure it out. Just believe in yourself."

"Is that what Nate is telling you to do?"

Mia hesitated before answering. Nate was a treacherous topic for her to discuss with Ivy. "It's the message of every positive affirmation ever written. Believe in yourself. Do what you love."

"Are you doing what you love?"

"Sure."

"I mean with me."

"You're my sister. I love being with you."

"I bet you'd love it more if you were with Nate."

Mia sensed the mines beneath her feet, and stepped carefully. "I've enjoyed working with him at the studio. I'm learning a lot. It's something I could see myself doing in the future."

It was the closest Mia had come to sharing her aspirations with Ivy. That she'd dared to confess something so personal terrified her. Ivy didn't like change and might view her twin's dream of having her own career as a threat.

"I wasn't talking about working at the studio. I was talking about Nate himself. You like him." Ivy's voice had taken on a coolness that made Mia shiver. "You like him a lot."

With a shaky laugh that wouldn't fool anyone, Mia said, "Everybody likes Nate."

"But everybody's not sleeping with him." Ivy's eyes glittered in the dim light. "You know he's using you, right?"

"I'm not sleeping with him." How many times had she lied to Ivy to keep her sister in the dark about Nate? A hundred? More? When was she planning to stop? Mia's chest tightened. She was barely able to draw breath enough to defend Nate. "And he's not like that."

"Did you do it because you knew I liked him? Have you been saying bad things to him about me? Is that why he criticized everything I did in the studio? I'm trying really hard to make him happy, but nothing makes him look at me the way he looks at you."

How did Nate look at her? "We're colleagues," Mia said. "That makes things easy between us. With you he's pushing so he can get the best possible song. It might seem like he's not happy, but he thinks this will be some of the best work you've done."

But Ivy wasn't listening to her. Mia had seen that look before. She got up and went to Ivy's purse. Her sister noticed what she was doing and protested. Mia ignored her and started digging through the bag, unsurprised when she came up with a small bag of pills.

"Who gave you these? Skylar or Riley?"

Ivy stuck her lower lip out and stared mutinously at Mia. "Give me those. It's none of your business."

"What's the matter with you?" Sorrow and rage collided inside Mia's chest. "I thought you were done taking prescription meds. Damn it, Ivy."

"I just need something to take the edge off after being in the studio all day. It's exhausting and the pressure… You just don't understand."

"I understand that you almost died because you were taking this stuff."

Mia took the bag into the bathroom and dumped

the contents into the toilet. When she turned, her sister was glaring at her from the doorway.

"You had no right." Ivy's voice slashed at her.

Discovering a bag of pills in her sister's possession both angered and frightened Mia. "I'm your sister and I love you. I'm always going to do what's best for you. Even if you hate me for it."

"It's your fault, you know. The reason I have the pills. You haven't been around for me lately."

"I'm with you all day at the studio and when you're working with Melody on the songs you're planning to record." Mia was having trouble catching her breath. She hated conflict and usually gave in to whatever Ivy wanted, but not when it came to her addiction. "The only time I'm not around is when you go out with Skylar and Riley. They're bad news, Ivy."

"They're fun." Ivy scrubbed the tears from her cheeks and shook her head. "I can't have any fun without you being all over me. You used to be fun. We used to hang out."

"That's not my fault." Mia's temper flared at the unfair accusation. It hurt that the two of them had stopped spending time together as sisters and friends. "You're the one who treats me more like an employee than your sister."

"You left me to go to high school."

Mia regarded Ivy in dumb silence. "You were in a show on Broadway. I wanted to be normal." Because she'd been just an average kid with no particular talent or ambition.

If Ivy had never become a pop star, Mia might have ended up like Eva, in a job she loved far from the music industry with its bright lights and soul-crushing pressure to make it big.

"You don't think that's what I wanted?" Ivy's pupils were like pinpoints, something Mia had learned to watch for. "To go to school with my friends and just worry about passing a chemistry test or what boy might think I'm cute?"

"So why didn't you say no?" Though Mia asked the question, she already knew the answer.

"You think it's because I love all the money and fame."

"I do. Ever since we were kids you always needed to be the center of attention."

"It gets old. Sometimes all I want is to be invisible."

"So quit."

"And do what?" Ivy glared at her. "I don't write music like you do. All I have is my voice and this body."

Mia wished her sister could look beyond show business. "What about going to college. You could get a degree. Or you're passionate about fashion. Start a clothing line."

"Sure." Ivy gave a bitter laugh. "Like Dad would let me quit singing and acting to become a fashion designer."

"You don't have to quit. Do both. See how it goes." For the first time in what felt like forever Mia saw the old Ivy peering out at her. She impulsively took her sister's hands. "Why don't we take Saturday and go do something fun? Just you and me. Like when we were kids and we used to sneak off to the park."

"I'm flying to LA with Skylar and Riley tomorrow to meet with the guy who is going to manufacture their line of purses."

"Tomorrow?" Why hadn't she been told any of this? "But you're scheduled in the studio tomorrow. When are you coming back?"

"I don't know. Skylar and Riley really need my help."

"And by help you mean they want you to invest money." If Mia had disliked Skylar and Riley before, the discovery of the pills made things so much worse.

"I don't care what you think." Ivy glared at her. "I'm going."

"Then I'll go with you." If Ivy was taking painkillers again, Mia really couldn't afford to let her sister go back to LA without her. "I'll message Nate and explain everything."

Well, not everything. She'd shared a lot of her secrets with him, but couldn't tell him her fears about Ivy without explaining about Ivy's near death overdose.

"Sure, whatever. But do it somewhere else. I'm tired and I just want to sleep."

"Then you're not going out tonight?"

"Geez, Mia. It's only seven. Nothing gets going

around here until at least midnight." And then Ivy lay on her bed and buried her face in a pillow.

After covering her with a throw, Mia took the now cool cup of tea and went to her bedroom to Skype with Nate. To her surprise, he was fine with the change of plans. He told her he'd head up to LA as well to meet with Trent, and would arrange for Ivy to do a bit of recording at West Coast Records with a producer friend of his so they could keep the schedule moving forward.

By the time Mia signed off an hour later, she was feeling a whole lot better. Nate had that effect on her. But her equanimity lasted only until she went to check on Ivy and found her sister's room in an uproar of rejected outfits, but otherwise empty.

Mia hesitated just a minute before starting a systematic search through Ivy's room. The last time her sister had given into her addiction, she'd squirrel away pills in all sorts of places. Mentally crossing her fingers that she wouldn't find anything, Mia began going through Ivy's drawers and closet. After forty-five minutes of searching, she'd unearthed no contraband, but that didn't mean Ivy couldn't hit up Skylar or Riley tonight.

Mia would have to keep a close eye on her sister to avoid a repeat of the relapse that had happened three years ago, while Ivy was on her first concert tour. Mia had been in LA working on a demo for one of the songs Ivy hadn't wanted to record. Preoccupied by the opportunity to have a career as a songwriter,

Mia hadn't been paying attention to her sister and Ivy had started taking pills again.

Sometimes it seemed that every time Mia tried to grab something for herself, Ivy found a way to spoil it. Which explained why keeping quiet about her relationship with Nate was so important. But at what cost? The question roused a host of emotions ranging from frustration to guilt. She'd already lost Nate to her sister's demanding personality.

Was she planning on sacrificing her entire future to it, as well? How long could she live in Ivy's shadow before dissatisfaction with her situation turned love into animosity? Choosing her sister over Nate had been hard the first time, even though she'd known him only a short while and could dismiss their fling as a tour romance. But now that she was working with him every day and accepting his help to develop her music, she was discovering richer layers to her feelings for him. Not sexual or even professional, but a complicated stew of romance, friendship and respect.

He was a brilliant musician and a wonderful man. When the time came to choose, how was she going to give him up again?

Six

Nate glanced Mia's way a hundred times during their drive to Santa Monica, where they were having dinner with Trent and Savannah. She looked beautiful in a navy-and-white abstract print sundress, paired with sandals and wavy beach hair. For a dramatic evening look, she'd applied eye shadow and red lipstick. He couldn't keep his eyes off her.

As he pulled into the parking lot, Mia gave the restaurant a doubtful look. "Are you sure this is a business meeting?"

He nodded, playing innocent when she frowned. He knew what she was thinking, but it wasn't really a double date. Just a quiet dinner with two couples, at a seaside restaurant with lots of good food and wine. Nope. Not a double date at all.

"It seems a little…"

He fitted the car into a parking spot and cut the engine. *"Out-of-the-way?"*

"I was thinking more in terms of romantic."

"Now that you mention it, I see what you mean. But I didn't pick it. Trent did. I think it might be date night for him and Savannah. That's not a problem, is it?"

"Sitting across the table from a newly engaged couple won't bother me a bit."

"Good. I wouldn't want you to get any ideas."

Mia shook her head. "I wouldn't dream of it."

They were fifteen minutes early for the reservation, but the hostess seated them at a wonderful table overlooking the Santa Monica pier and the ocean. The sun had already dipped below the horizon and the sky was saturated with rich gold, red and deep blue.

"Tell me more about Trent and Savannah." Mia's eyes held a wistful glow as she turned from the view. "Start with why they both have the same last name if they're only engaged."

"Savannah is Trent's former sister-in-law."

Mia's eyes widened adorably. "That has to be a tricky situation."

"It's quite complicated. They've known each other since Savannah was a kid. She came to live with her aunt, who happened to be the Caldwells' housekeeper, after her mom died and her father couldn't take care of her. From what Melody tells me, Sa-

vannah had a thing for Trent for a long time. When she went off to model in New York City he went out to visit her and they began to..." Nate paused and thought for a moment. *"Date."*

"Why the pause?"

"I don't think Trent realized how he felt about her until after they broke up and she married his brother."

"So why did she marry him? To get back at Trent?"

"That's not her style. She was pregnant and Rafe wanted a legitimate heir to carry on the Caldwell name. He was dying when he married her, but no one knew."

"How old is her son?"

"Just turned a year. And the boy is Trent's. How that happened is also complicated, but let's just say Trent was a huge idiot for ever letting her go."

"Did Trent know about the baby before she married his brother?"

Nate shook his head. *"I think if they'd been able to talk to each other when she found out she was pregnant they might have saved themselves a lot of heartache."*

"Why didn't she tell him?"

"That would be a good question to ask her. I don't honestly know."

\"I'm glad Trent and Savannah found each other again." Mia paused while Nate ordered a bottle of pinot grigio from the waiter. "I don't remember Trent being a part of West Coast Records when Ivy signed with them. How long has he been involved? It's his family business, isn't it?"

"That's another complicated thing. Trent and his father never got along, so he wasn't involved in the record label. His brother, Rafe took over when their father retired, and mismanaged an already floundering company."

"My dad told me there were rumors that artists weren't being paid. That never happened with Ivy, but she was one of their bestselling artists."

"Trent brought in auditors to look over the books. There was some embezzling on top of everything else. Hopefully, within the next six months everything will get straightened out and people will be paid what they're owed."

The waiter brought the wine, and as it was being poured, Trent and Savannah arrived at the table. Quick introductions were made and the newly engaged couple sat down.

"You two are early," Trent said, his gaze sliding between Nate and Mia.

"They didn't have a baby to get ready for bed," Savannah said.

"How is your throat?" Trent asked. "Are you speaking yet?"

Nate shook his head and glanced at Mia.

"I'm his voice."

Savannah's eyes widened. "How does that work?"

Nate demonstrated. *"I want to lick every inch of your body."*

"He just said you look lovely and asked how your son is."

"I don't think that's what he said." Savannah laughed. "You just turned bright red. Did he say something naughty?"

Trent cocked his head and regarded his smirking business partner. "So are you two...?"

"Lovers?" He nodded.

"No."

Nate had little trouble conveying his feelings on that situation. *"Not at the moment."*

Savannah grinned. "This feels a little bit like watching a silent movie without subtitles."

"We're being rude," Mia said, shooting Nate a severe look.

"Tell them the truth. It won't go anywhere."

She gave a big sigh. "Nate and I became romantically involved while on tour, but nobody knows that."

"Because?" Savannah prompted.

Nate began to sign, but Mia ignored him. "I work for my sister and she wouldn't be happy if I was dating Nate."

"Because?" It was Trent who prompted this time.

Mia looked as if she wished the floor would open up and swallow her. "My sister can be a bit needy."

The sign Nate made needed no translation.

"So you're not allowed to date?" Savannah asked. "That seems a bit much."

"It's not that I can't date." Although from what she'd told Nate, her sister had a knack for ruining every chance at romance that came Mia's way. "It's more that I don't have much time for a life outside my work."

"Mia is a fantastic songwriter. I found out on tour that she wrote all the songs Ivy claimed to have written from her first two albums." Nate finished signing and gave her a hard look until she translated his words.

Trent gave her an equally hard look as he listened, but there was regret in there, as well. "You weren't given credit? How did that happen?"

"I don't know," Mia said. "When the first albums came out I wasn't mentioned at all. When I asked my dad about it, he said it was a group decision. They thought it looked better if Ivy was writing her own music instead of some nobody."

From the throb in Mia's voice, the slight continued to pain her.

"If it was something that happened because of my family's mismanagement of the West Coast label, I would be happy to set the record straight."

"No." Mia added a head shake for emphasis. "It would cause too much upheaval. My family would never forgive me if word got out."

Trent nodded. "If anyone understands how complicated family and business can be it's me. You have my word that this stays here."

"Thank you."

Mia gave Trent a wobbly smile and it hit Nate hard. He wanted badly to be able to make everything right for her, but she'd never let him. The best he could hope would be to get her away from Ivy so that her future looked brighter.

They dined on the fresh catch of the day and went through several bottles of wine. Trent, Savannah and Mia carried the conversation. Nate enjoyed his forced muteness and spent most of the dinner watching Mia's confidence bloom beneath his friends' attention.

"Dessert?" Nate asked as the waiter cleared the plates. He wanted to prolong the night as long as possible.

Savannah looked regretful. "I wish we could, but we promised the sitter we'd get home by ten."

Nate turned to Mia, but she was shaking her head. *"How about a walk on the beach?"*

She glanced out the window at the dark water. He knew she loved the ocean. They'd sneaked off to the beach a couple times while touring Australia. He would've liked to steal her away for some snorkeling along the Great Barrier Reef, but the schedule had been too tight for that sort of excursion.

"A short one. If I'm too late Ivy will wonder why."

After settling the bill the two couples separated in the parking lot. Mia maintained her smile as she stripped off her sandals and put them in the car. The temperature had dipped into the upper fifties, but the breeze blowing off the Pacific was light.

Nate took her hand and they made their way toward the sand. As they crossed the broad expanse, he revisited how easy it was to be with Mia. She had an ability to stay tranquil no matter how crazy the people around her became. No doubt it was a trait she'd cultivated in dealing with her sister's demanding ways.

Mia didn't expect conversation or feel compelled to fill silences with chatter. Even before his surgery, they'd spent long silent hours enjoying each other's company, physically connected by the touch of her foot on his thigh or his shoulder against hers, or at opposite ends of a room, content to occupy the same space.

If it weren't for Mia's peculiar attachment to being her sister's assistant, he could've delighted in having found the perfect woman. Instead his patience was worn to the thinness of onion skin by his constant need to resist the craving to pull Mia into his arms and kiss her. He was tired of pretending his interest in her was professional.

Fingers knitted together, they walked at the water's edge, heading away from the bright lights of the Santa Monica pier. The quarter moon gave them enough light to see by. Nate stopped and used Mia's momentum to turn her into his arms. Sliding his hand into her hair, he cupped her cheek and brought his lips to hers.

She tasted of the peppermint candy she'd snagged on the way out of the restaurant. When he licked at her lips, they parted for him, and he swept his tongue against hers, stealing her breath and the last bit of the candy disk. He'd always been good with words when it came to writing music, but this rush of emotion that hit him whenever he put his arms around her smothered his ability to form cohesive thought.

"I have a few more hours before Ivy will be home," she murmured against his cheek as he grazed his lips down her neck. She trembled as he nipped her skin. "Feel like going back to your hotel? I'm dying to be alone with you."

Nate didn't bother signing his answer. He grabbed her by the hand and pulled her toward the car. Mia laughed at his eagerness. It matched the impatience burning in her chest. Why hadn't she said something sooner? They'd wasted fifteen minutes on this walk.

Nate had one hand on the steering wheel and caressed her shoulder with the other while he drove. There was little conversation on the trip back into the city. It gave Mia time to think about what was to come and to work herself into a fine state of frenzied anticipation.

At the hotel, Nate turned his car over to the valet. When he would've put his arm around Mia for the walk through the hotel lobby, she shook her head.

"We can't be seen together like that," she cautioned, thinking what would happen if a picture got out of the two of them linked romantically. "I don't want to show up on social media and invite speculation."

"I think you overestimate my star power."

Mia rolled her eyes. The man had no idea how incredible he was. "I think you underestimate it."

"I'm pretty low-key off tour. And I don't really have one of those faces that everybody knows."

"Are you kidding? You're gorgeous." She covered her mouth with her hand and laughed self-consciously. "I don't know why I'm embarrassed admitting that to you. You already know how I feel."

"I'm not really sure I do." Nate frowned down at her for a long moment.

They joined several other hotel guests in the elevator and got out on the twelfth floor. He took her hand and brought it to his lips. The way he watched her turned her bones to mush. She spent so much time hiding how he made her feel. It was a relief to let her emotions shine.

His eyes widened. *"I never thought I'd see you look at me like that again."*

"I've been fighting this for two months," she murmured as they walked toward his suite. "It's been hell wanting you and knowing—" Her voice broke. The last thing he deserved was to hear her say again that she'd chosen being there for her sister over him.

His fingers tightened against hers as he slid the key card into the electronic lock. As soon as they crossed the threshold he kicked the door closed, gathered her into his arms and kissed her. Mia sighed against his mouth, her lips parting to welcome the plunge of his tongue. She filled her fingers with his soft wavy hair and held him close.

I love you. The words reverberated in her mind, but she didn't dare say them out loud. As much as she wanted him, wanted this, she couldn't commit to anything beyond this night. Soon she would have to consider Nate's place in her life. This connection between them had grown so fast and Mia wasn't accustomed to recklessly throwing herself into any situation. And then there were the doubts that rose after Ivy voiced her opinion about Mia not belonging in the limelight by his side.

Mia took Nate's hand and drew him toward the suite's bedroom. He deserved someone beautiful and confident to walk the red carpet and make other public appearances with him. Mia was too used to hiding in the background, and she knew he wanted to partner in everything private and public. But with his hands sweeping down her spine, his palms sliding over her butt cheeks to lift her against his hard body, it was hard to think about all the reasons she wasn't right for him.

"I'm going to do all the talking for you tonight," she told him, panting as his lips found the sensitive skin on the side of her neck. "You just tell me what to say and I'll say it."

There was a mischievous glint in the depths of Nate's gray eyes as he made an okay sign. He snagged the hem of her dress and skimmed it up her body. The cool air struck her overheated skin and Mia shivered. For a couple seconds the cotton material tangled in her hair as it went over her head and she was blinded. The loss of her sight awakened her sense of smell and she breathed in Nate's familiar scent of soap and aftershave.

Immediately she was transported back to that night in Sydney. She'd been a little intimidated by the discrepancy between their levels of sexual experience and what he might expect of her. And then she'd forgotten to be nervous as his mouth traveled over her body and he introduced her to pleasure she'd never known. After having nearly two months to relive that night over and over, Mia was more than ready to do to him all the things she'd been dreaming about.

His shirt followed her dress to the floor. Once his gorgeous chest was bared to her eyes, she went after his pants with a vengeance. Teeth gritted in concentration, she worked his belt free and had her hands on his zipper when he stopped her.

"What are you doing?" She tugged, trying to free herself from his grip. "I need you naked."

Nate set his forehead against hers and brought her hands to his lips. His breath puffed against her skin as he feathered kisses across her knuckles. Then he turned her in his arms and shifted so they were facing the mirror.

"Before we do this, I want you to know it's never been just about sex for me."

"I know." She relaxed against Nate's strong torso. The hard ridge of his erection nudged against her backside and she resisted the urge to rub against him. "But can't we talk about this later?"

"Now. It's important you understand how much I need you in my life. This isn't something I'm doing lightly. Can you say the same?"

"If you're going to ask me to choose you right now, I can't. Is it possible for you to accept that I care about you and want this to work between us? I'm not leading you on, but I need time to sort everything out."

"You're asking me to be patient."

"And I know it's a lot. You're so wonderful and I don't want to hurt you."

"I wish I could tell you I will make it easy on you, but I'm a selfish jerk who wants you all to himself." He met her eyes in the mirror and gave her wolfish grin. *"Now repeat after me..."* He began simultaneously signing and caressing her body to act out his words.

"I love your breasts and the way your nipples go hard when I touch them," she translated, quaking in reaction to his touch. "Nate, you're killing me with this."

He stopped signing long enough to pop the clasp of her strapless bra. Mia watched it slide off her breasts and hit the floor. Next he skimmed his fingers beneath the elastic of her panties and sent those plunging to the floor, too. Mia stepped out of them. Although she was no stranger to her naked body reflected in the mirror, seeing Nate's large hand fanned over her stomach was an erotic image she'd never forget.

"Keep going."

"I can't wait to taste you." A vivid blush dotted her cheeks as she repeated what Nate had signed. "I love how sensitive you are. It makes me crazy to hear you moan."

He trailed the tips of his fingers along her neck and into the hollow of her throat, all the while watching her in the mirror. She half closed her eyes as each of her senses demanded her attention. The silky drag of his lips across her shoulder competed with the tantalizing view of his fingers circling her belly button before skimming downward.

"Nate." His name was a plea as she shifted her hips, seeking the promise of greater pleasure beneath his hands. "Yes."

"Yes, what?"

"Am I ready for you?" she repeated, her voice a husky moan. "The answer is yes."

He laughed, a brief huff of air against her neck. *"I'm ready for you, too. Can't you feel it?"* He rocked his hips forward and drove his erection against her.

"Then what are you waiting for?"

She dropped her hand to his thigh and slid her palm along the sinewy length. His muscles bunched and jumped beneath her touch.

"I like taking my time with you," Mia repeated, watching as he lifted his fingers to her breasts and brushed the aching tips. She arched her back. "Later you can take your time. Now I want you to make me come."

"My pleasure."

While one hand cupped her breast, the other slid between her legs and dipped into the heat generated by his tantalizing caresses and sexy words. He touched her with tender confidence, sliding his finger around the sensitive nub until she quaked and groaned.

"Oh, yes. There."

He knew exactly what turned her on.

With his hands otherwise occupied and his voice out of commission he had no way to convey how he was feeling, but Mia could guess from the wonder that bloomed across his features and the ragged nature of his breathing.

"Kiss me," she pleaded. Although it pained her to pull his hands from between her legs, she needed his mouth on hers.

She turned to face him and his hands slid into her hair, fingers pressing into her scalp as he tilted her head and brought his mouth to hers. She gasped at the joy and welcomed the plunge of his tongue, meeting it with her own. Her toes curled at the shudder that ran through him when her hands smoothed over his back and down his spine.

During their night together on tour, Nate had proved to be very vocal in bed, crooning encouragement and telling her how she tasted and felt. She could tell his need to remain silent was very frustrating, because his hands tracked over her bare skin with feverish longing.

Mia broke off the kiss and pushed him to arm's length. "Pants off. Now."

With a snappy salute, Nate made short work of his zipper and sent his trousers sliding down his legs. Mia didn't wait for him to take care of his boxer briefs. Her fingers were already on the waistband, yanking them down to free him. His breath was ragged as his fingers formed the sign for a curse word, making Mia smile.

"Get ready," she said. "You haven't yet begun to swear."

She dropped to her knees before him and took him into her mouth before he had a chance to realize what she intended. She closed her eyes to savor the warm, smooth skin stretched over his rigid erection. His hips jerked as she rolled her tongue around him and smiled as his fingers bit down on her shoulder. It must be killing him to remain silent. As much as she didn't want to cause damage to his voice, she knew the fight to stay quiet would only enhance the tension building in him.

He double tapped her shoulder, indicating he wanted her attention. She lifted her gaze and met his eyes, letting him see how much she enjoyed what she was doing to him.

"You're killing me."

In answer, she took him deeper, using her hand at the base of his erection to provide sensation along the full length of his shaft. She thought about all the things they hadn't done that first night, and not getting to do this for him had been her biggest regret.

The tension in his body built as she worked her mouth on him, but even as his pleasure soared, he broke free and pulled her to her feet. For a long moment he held her cradled against his chest, her ear atop his pounding heart. When he seemed to get himself back under control, he pushed her to arm's length and signed, *"When I come it will be inside you."*

She shivered and took his hand, walking backward toward the bed. Nate reached into the nightstand and pulled out a condom. He brushed her hands aside when she tried to help him. With him otherwise occupied, she let her fingers drift over the taut muscles of his shoulder and biceps.

Once he finished putting on the protection, he turned to her and pointed to the bed. *"Up you go. I'm going to make love to you now."*

"That sounds about perfect."

She shifted onto the middle of the mattress and he stalked right after her, his hot gaze raking over her.

"You are so beautiful." His fingertips grazed her breast, circling the puckered tip.

"So are you." The words were barely a whisper as he closed his mouth over her nipple and sucked hard.

She gasped, the sound escaping her like a half cry as his tongue flicked the sensitive bud. She skidded her fingers along his cheeks and down his shoulders to his back. Muscles bunched and loosened beneath her touch as she investigated each rib and bump in his spine. How often had she watched him move around the stage, his long lithe body filled with such energy and emotion, and wondered what it would be like to be up against his rock-hard abs, a heartbeat away from those mobile, smiling lips?

And then she had been. After one of the shows, Nate had drawn her into a dressing room and kissed her. It was like being embraced by a power line. All the hyped up energy he'd received from performing had translated into a passionate kiss. It had been crazy magic.

He grabbed her hand and now pulled it to his mouth. His eyes captured hers as if asking for permission. Her voice was gone so she nodded.

"I want all of you. Right now. As deep and hard as you want it. Fast or slow," she finally said.

Nate closed his eyes and set his forehead against hers. He gave her the sweetest kiss on the corner of her mouth. *"I don't deserve you."*

You deserve so much better than me. She didn't dare speak the words for fear it would ruin the moment. Instead, she framed his face with her hands and brought his lips to hers. They kissed and passion overwhelmed them once more. He shifted to lie between her spread legs. Once again his fingers drifted between her folds and found her wet and aching. A shudder raged through him as he slid a finger inside her, making her moan. Mia's hips lifted off the bed.

She grabbed his wrist, intent on doing…something to satisfy the tension building inside her. Her gaze flicked to his face and she found him watching what he was doing to her. Her heart tripped and stopped at the level of joy mingling with lust in his expression. And then she was over the edge, her hips bucking as she rode the release Nate had brought to her body.

She barely noticed when he guided himself into position, but as she experienced the last spasms of her orgasm, Nate drove his hips against hers, filling her.

Seven

Air hissed between his teeth as he stopped moving. He was now fully seated inside her and he took a second to appreciate the moment with this spectacular woman. Mia's internal muscles clenched around him as aftershocks reverberated through her. He stroked strands of hair off her cheek and peered at her flushed face and passion-dazed eyes. She was beautiful and sweet. And all his.

She blew out a breath and lifted her gaze to his. He saw a hint of the shyness that always intrigued him. As if she couldn't quite believe he'd noticed her.

As if that was possible.

He raised his eyebrows in a silent question.

"I'm perfect. You're perfect. This—" Mia purred

as she ran the soles of her feet along Nate's thighs "—is perfect."

It was all he needed to hear. He began to move, pulling out slowly, before driving back in, loving the way her breath caught and her lashes fluttered. Two months without her was two months too long. Already he could feel pleasure tighten in a frantic ache that pulled him toward completion.

"Harder," she begged. Her nails dug into his back. The tiny pain shot straight to his groin. "Yes," she moaned as he picked up speed. "Like that."

Staying silent during sex was way more frustrating than anything he'd experienced in the last two weeks since his surgery. Curses flooded his mind as he sank into Mia's tight, hot body over and over. He wanted to tell her how good she felt. How she was unlike any woman he'd ever known. Instead, he kissed her, letting his mouth speak in other ways.

His orgasm was close, but he needed her to go first. As their breath rushed together in frantic pants, he slipped his hand between them and cupped her. She uttered a soft cry that sounded like a garbled version of his name and then threw her head back. Her muscles clamped down on him hard and she was going over the edge.

Nate kept himself from climaxing long enough to watch her, and then he couldn't hold it back any longer. He buried his face in her shoulder as his body exploded in pleasure. His lips moved, forming her name against her skin as he gave one final thrust and spilled himself inside her for what felt like endless seconds.

As he became aware of the room again, Nate rolled onto his side, taking her with him.

"Incredible," he signed.

"You can say that again."

He made the sign a second time and she laughed. Brushing aside a damp strand of hair, he made another sign. *"Stay."*

She shook her head. Already he could feel her starting to disengage.

"I can't."

He fought down his disappointment. *"An hour more?"*

When she gave a reluctant nod, he brought his lips to hers. It wasn't much time, but enough to make certain that the next time he asked her to stay, she'd have a much harder time refusing.

Club T's was in full swing when Ivy and three of her besties were escorted past the line of attractive twentysomethings waiting by the velvet ropes for their chance to get in. Mia trailed behind the group, anonymous and forgettable in a sleeveless black dress that skimmed her curves but left everything else to the imagination. In contrast, Ivy wore a red sequin romper with a plunging neckline that showed off her long legs, toned by hours of dance rehearsals and yoga.

The group bypassed the dance floor and headed

straight for the VIP area. The DJ was cranking great tunes and with Ivy preoccupied for the moment, Mia let herself fall a little behind.

Their private table was set up with bottles of vodka, champagne and assorted mixes. Flanked by her entourage, Ivy slipped into the booth. There was enough space between the couches and the table for the women to rock their hips to the music and fling their hair extensions around. Ivy was in high spirits, yelling that she loved every song that played.

Mia perched on the far end of the couch, suddenly overwhelmed. By the concussive beat. The dazzling light show. The hyped-up customers all around them, whooping, dancing and sucking up all the oxygen. Dizziness consumed her. Mia closed her eyes, wishing she were somewhere tranquil and quiet.

Someone shook her shoulder. Mia's eyes opened and she spied Ivy bent over the table and frowning at her.

"Did you order this?" Ivy demanded, pointing to the bottles. "It's Grey Goose. I wanted Belvedere."

"You always drink Grey Goose," Mia said, feeling very much like screaming.

"Not lately." Ivy rolled her eyes. "You never pay attention."

"I'll go find someone and get it fixed." Mia was glad for the chance to escape. "Be right back."

With the mixes disguising the taste of the liquor, Mia doubted whether Ivy could distinguish one type of vodka from another. Most often she made demands to remind everyone that she was the celebrity. Mia was probably one of the few people who recognized she did it out of insecurity.

And Ivy was feeling all too anxious at the moment. She was fighting the direction Nate wanted for her album and the stress had sent her running for the comfortable fog of prescription meds. This meant Mia needed to be more vigilant than ever. She just needed to get Ivy through the album and then her sister would calm down.

Mia headed to the first floor in search of a waitress and cleared up the vodka situation. She was standing on the edge of the dance floor, wondering if it would be possible to locate Nate in the crowd, when an arm came around her waist, startling her. Mia tensed, intending on twisting away, when a familiar cologne danced past her nostrils. She glanced down as Nate's hands moved.

"Relax. I've got you."

A thousand butterflies took flight in her stomach as he drew her into the crowd on the dance floor. Twisting, grinding bodies surrounded them, driving Mia against Nate so they had no choice but to touch. He turned her so her back rested against his chest and his hands could roam over her.

"I can't." But her words were lost to a groan as his lips trailed along her neck and his hot breath spilled across her skin. "Ivy and her friends are just…over…" She sucked in a jagged breath as his thumb grazed her nipple.

"Damn, I've missed you."

Me, too. She didn't bother with the words. Her muscles trembled as he grazed his hands up her sides and over her ribs, telling him everything he needed to know.

Earlier the music and crowd had bothered her. But away from Ivy and her friends, Mia wanted to get lost on the dance floor for an hour or two, gyrating with the rest of the crowd to the bass-heavy music until her feet had blisters on top of blisters and she was drenched with sweat. How long had it been since she'd done something fun or crazy just for herself?

Two days.

She shut her eyes, blocking out the million-dollar light show, and whisked back in time to the hotel suite and Nate's naked body sliding against her skin as they made love. Placing her hands over his, heat blazing in her cheeks, she pressed him closer.

His familiar scent wrapped around her and she filled her lungs until her chest ached. Nate's body aligned with hers was perfection. It banished her loneliness, stripped away her inhibitions and demolished her dependability until she became someone else. Someone who excited her. Someone filled with poignant emotions of such perfect joy that they terrified her.

That was why she'd broken off with Nate when the tour ended. She couldn't be two people. She had to choose. In the end, she'd shied away from embracing the daring, impulsive woman she became around

Nate and retreated back into the familiar territory of being Ivy's highly efficient, but mostly ignored PA.

Hips swaying in sync, Mia and Nate rocked to the music pouring over them, but all she could hear was the sound of her heart crying in joy. Nothing made her happier than being with Nate. But her life had never been about being happy. It had been about obligation, selflessness and patience.

Sleeping with Nate while in LA had been foolish and reckless, but she wouldn't trade it for anything.

Against her side, her purse buzzed, jolting Mia back to responsibility. She offered up a huge sigh and tugged Nate's hands away from her body. Turning, she signed.

"I have to go."

She made a fist with her right hand to form the letter *A* and then circled it clockwise against her chest twice. Her apology did little to ease the irritation that tightened his lips into a relentless line. Green and amber lights played over his face, highlighting his unhappy expression as he signed a rude response.

"Ivy will wonder where I am."

"I don't care."

"I know."

She grabbed his wrist and dragged him off the dance floor. She thought to leave him near the bar and return to Ivy, but he was on her heels as she ascended the stairs to the VIP section. At the top, Nate was hailed by a pair of tall men, Kyle Tailor, the third partner in Club T's, and Hunter Graves. In the last five years Hunter had become increasingly in demand as a DJ and a producer.

"You have company." Mia indicated the two tall men heading their way. "I should get back to Ivy."

"In a second. Come translate for me."

Before she could refuse, Nate caught her hand and towed her to meet the two men. Mia had never been formally introduced to either of them, but thanks to Melody she knew the story behind Kyle's annoyed frown.

Kyle was the first to speak. "Hey, Nate."

Hunter Graves stuck out his hand with a broad grin. "Good to see you. Kyle was just showing me around. This place is great."

Kyle checked his phone. "I have to take care of something," he said, sending a meaningful glance Nate's way, obviously eager to get away from the DJ. "You don't mind taking over for me, do you?"

As Kyle retreated down the stairs, Nate shook Hunter's hand and glanced at Mia as he indicated his throat.

"He had throat surgery," Mia said. She put out her hand. "I'm Mia Navarro, his translator."

"You're more than that," Nate signed, while she and Hunter shook hands.

"Nice to meet you," Hunter said. "I can't wait to get up there and spin for this crowd." He indicated the DJ booth that overlooked the dance floor. "They're on fire."

"We're glad to have you here," Mia repeated.

Hunter's eyes widened as he gazed from her to

Nate and back again. "You weren't kidding about the translating. That's cool. Your own secret language."

"It's been handy having her around the studio these last few weeks."

Mia translated what Nate signed, and then added her own two cents. "His handwriting is terrible. I don't know what would've happened if he'd been forced to write down everything he wanted to say."

Hunter laughed and Mia could see why Melody had been hung up on him for so long. His engaging grin made it easy to smile back. Nate nudged her with his elbow and she shot him a questioning glance.

"Stop flirting with him."

"Did Trent mention to you that I'm interested in booking some time in at Ugly Trout?" Hunter asked, his keen gaze missing little of their exchange.

Nate nodded.

"I've got a couple artists I've started working with and thought it might be good to have them come to Vegas while I'm here."

"Speaking of artists," Mia said, "Ivy's here tonight. Why don't we head over there and you can say hi." Mia glanced at Nate as she finished speaking and sent a mischievous grin his way.

There'd been a very brief flirtation between Hunter and Ivy a year earlier. Hunter might be the perfect anecdote for Ivy's stress. If nothing else, he'd be a good distraction. Although Hunter liked to play as hard as he worked, he was an advocate for clean living. Maybe reconnecting with him would convince Ivy to send Skylar and Riley packing.

"It would be great to see her," Hunter said. "Lead the way."

As he gestured for Hunter to follow Mia, Nate could tell she had something up her sleeve. By the time he reached the table, introductions were being made and Ivy's girlfriends fell over themselves swarming the DJ. Not only was Hunter charismatic and good-looking, but his net worth was in the high seven figures, making him a player worth pursuing.

Ivy didn't seem to be as impressed, but she was the star and, as always, wanted everyone to know it. But when Hunter gave her his best wicked grin, she thawed and patted the cushion beside her.

Mia signed an explanation. *"They had a brief thing and I think she still likes him."*

Now Nate understood. *"So he's a distraction?"*

Her smile was all the answer he needed and it gave him an idea. Maybe having Hunter in Las Vegas was going to be a good thing, after all. Having him spend time with Ivy might kill two birds with one stone.

The friction between Nate and Ivy in the studio meant that recording the album wasn't going smoothly. He could put it down to artistic differences, but more likely she'd picked up on his disgust for the way she treated Mia, or any number of the other things that irritated him about her. Whatever the cause, the chemistry between them was all bad.

Nate had heard nothing but good things about Hunter as a producer, and he suspected the DJ would love an opportunity to work with Ivy. Maybe he'd have better luck dealing with the pop princess. And if Hunter was reluctant to tackle Ivy's album, maybe he'd be interested in her personally. She was beautiful and talented enough to appeal to him.

And that was the second reason to push them together. Weeks earlier Trent had signed Hunter to a one year contract as a DJ with Club T's, which meant Hunter was going to be spending a lot more time in Las Vegas. While he promised to be a huge draw on Sunday nights, Nate was worried this might further disrupt Melody and Kyle's relationship.

A year earlier Melody had been dating Hunter. They'd been together eighteen months and she found him lacking in the commitment department.

Kyle was Trent's best friend since high school and had always treated his buddy's little sister like family. After listening to Melody complain about her relationship woes, Kyle insisted that if Hunter thought he had competition, he would stop taking her for granted.

At some point during their six-week ruse, both of them got caught up in their pretend romance. But it wasn't until Hunter came to his senses and realized he was about to lose Melody that she and Kyle admitted to each other that they'd fallen in love.

For a while things were going great between them. But then Melody had gone on tour with Nate and the separation had taken its toll on the fledgling romance. Melody and Kyle were committed to making the long-distance thing work right up until Melody got caught by the paparazzi coming out of a New York City club hand-in-hand with Hunter.

The whole incident had been innocent enough. He'd taken her hand to keep from being separated in the crush leaving the club, but there was too much history between Melody and Hunter for Kyle to dismiss the episode.

Seeing that Ivy was utterly absorbed in the DJ, Nate caught Mia by the arm and drew her away.

"Where are we going?" she asked, as he guided her toward the stairs once more.

"Somewhere I can put my hands all over you."

"I really shouldn't be gone for very long."

"Hunter will keep her busy. Let's you and I find a private spot and make out."

She glanced back over her shoulder. "Twenty minutes. No more."

He could definitely work with that. Nate led her through the club to a discreet door that opened into a nondescript hallway. Mia blinked in the sudden brightness of the florescent lighting.

"Where are we going?"

"Somewhere we won't be interrupted." He pulled out his phone and shot Kyle a quick text, warning his business partner that he was going to use Trent's office for a private meeting and didn't want to be disturbed.

While Nate had mentioned to Kyle that he was seeing someone, he hadn't revealed that it was Mia. It wasn't that Nate was keeping her a secret—Melody and Trent knew—but the friendship between the two men was strained because of what was happening between Kyle and Melody.

Nate hadn't exactly taken sides, but Melody was one of his favorite people and she wasn't the one behaving like an idiot. The way Kyle had reacted after her New York club incident with Hunter made Nate feel less than friendly toward his business partner.

Relationships weren't always easy—Nate could attest to that with what was going on between him and Mia—but when you loved someone, you should trust them. And from what he was seeing of Kyle, the guy was worrying more about guarding his heart than opening it to Melody.

And that was the last thought Nate intended to have on that subject for the next hour. He ushered Mia in and closed and locked the door to Trent's office, sealing them inside the space. He didn't bother to turn on the overhead lights. One wall of floor-to-ceiling monitors, tuned to various locations around the club, provided enough light to highlight the wet bar, Trent's neat desk and, most important for Nate's purposes, a comfortable couch.

"Now that you have me here," Mia said, dropping her purse on an end table, "what do you plan to do?"

Was she kidding? He swooped her into his arms and deposited her on the couch. His lips found hers even as her fingers skimmed his suit coat off his shoulders. Fortunately, he wasn't wearing a tie and she was making quick work of the buttons on his dark gray shirt. He barely restrained a groan as her palms slid over his abs and skated around to his back.

As much as he enjoyed that her skill as a translator kept her at his side, he really wanted his voice back so he could tell her all the delicious, wicked things he intended to do to her. Although he could easily spend the near future indulging in one slow, drugging kiss after another, he was afraid they might interrupted by yet another summons from Ivy.

He kissed his way down her neck and across her shoulder. The dress she wore zipped up the back and he cursed himself for not taking it off her before he got her onto the couch. He slid his hand up her bare thigh, hearing her gasp as he hooked his fingertips into her panties and gave a tug. With a little help from her, he got her underwear off. Then she eased the hem of her dress upward until she'd exposed her lower half.

Smiling at the gorgeous picture she made, Nate settled his shoulders between her thighs and pressed his mouth against her. Everything about the moment was perfect, from the way she tasted to the sweet, mewling sounds of pleasure that escaped her lips as he pushed her to the edge of desire and held her there.

She clutched and released his hair as her thighs began to tremble and her back arched. She sighed his name on a ragged breath as he slid two fingers inside her and made her climax. Her hips lifted as she came, body tensing as her release crashed over her. As always he marveled at the power and duration of her orgasm. The only thing he enjoyed more than watching her come was being with her when it happened.

Mia went limp beneath him. "That was just… wow." She panted. "Give me a second and I'll return the favor."

Nate grinned as he stripped off his clothes, slipped on a condom and returned to the couch. Mia had been watching him the whole time, grinning like a satisfied cat.

"You are gorgeous, do you know that?" she murmured as he lay flat on his back and repositioned her so that she straddled him.

"So are you, but I like you better naked." He reached behind her and managed to unzip her dress. In seconds it was on the floor. Her bra followed. He traced her breasts with his fingertips and smiled. *"Much better."*

She lifted her hips and closed her hand around his erection. Nate hissed between his teeth, but before he could react further, she'd settled herself over him. While stars exploded in his vision, Mia leaned forward and kissed him, with such tenderness Nate's heart nearly stopped.

"No," she corrected him, sucking his lower lip between her teeth. "This is much better."

"I stand corrected."

With a husky laugh, she began to move. And suddenly they had no further need for words.

Eight

Five days following that epic night with Nate at Club T's, Mia decided she couldn't put off taking a pregnancy test any longer. While it wasn't unusual for her to miss an occasional period due to stress, or if she was doing a lot of traveling with Ivy, it was over two months since that night in Sydney and time she pulled her head out of the sand.

Part of Mia recognized the old adage that what you don't know can't hurt you. Until she took the test, she didn't have to think about the future. But each day she delayed, the worry consumed her more, and she couldn't decide if her queasy stomach was morning sickness, plain old anxiety or a little of both. Today, however, she'd decided to stop procrastinating.

It was the morning of the AMAs and Ivy was

scheduled for a video interview at eight thirty. As soon as her twin slapped on the headphones, Mia made a break for the door. In ten minutes she'd bought the pregnancy test and returned to the television studio. Although taking the test in the bathroom there wasn't ideal, it was better than taking it at home.

She now had ten more minutes until Ivy would be done. Fortunately, she had a full bladder and the test took only three minutes to show results.

She sat on the toilet to wait. Head down, eyes closed, Mia sorted through her tangled emotions for a bright thread of certainty. How did she want things to turn out?

Pregnant? Joy at the possibility filled her like a crystal-pure note perfectly sung. But almost immediately anxiety rose up in her, drowning out the happy emotion. If she was pregnant, her life as she knew it was over. Nothing could possess her to keep being Ivy's assistant, and when Ivy found out who'd fathered her child, Mia would probably find her relationship with her sister over, as well.

And what if she wasn't pregnant? She'd feel a mixture of relief and disappointment. Everything would be easier. She wouldn't have to change a single thing about her life.

But was that really what she wanted? How long did she think she was going to be Ivy's assistant? Was she going to be forty or fifty and still following her sister around? Fetching for her. Putting up with her insecurities. With no husband and children and few friends.

Tears welled up in her eyes. She fought them off by taking several deep breaths and stabbing her fingernails into her palms. A baby would change everything. She could make a case for choosing her child over her sister. The guilt her parents heaped on her shoulders would lose its power.

Three minutes had never felt longer. Mia watched the seconds tick by on her cell phone; she'd started the stopwatch as soon as she took the test. While the seconds ticked off, she stayed in the stall, too afraid to stand in the bathroom proper and get caught with a pregnancy test in her hand. Not that anyone would know who she was or care what she was doing. Sometimes being invisible was nice. But there was that tiny chance that someone would be interested in what was going on and that information could leave the bathroom and cause her a lot of trouble.

When the time was up, Mia found herself unable to look at the test. She sat with it in her lap, the indicator facing downward. She didn't need to look to see the answer. She already knew. She was pregnant. Her phone buzzed, scaring her. She dropped the test. It clattered to the floor and landed faceup.

These days the tests were easy to read. No more questionable results. Depending on which one you chose, there was a line, the word *yes* or the word *pregnant*. In Mia's case it was "pregnant." She swallowed a hysterical laugh. Her whole life had just changed inside the bathroom of a TV station.

No, that wasn't quite true. Her whole life had changed the day she'd met Nate.

Mia had about thirty seconds to absorb the reality of her situation before the bathroom door opened and two women entered with a gust of animated chatter. She recognized the voices and quickly snatched the pregnancy test off the ground and dropped it into her work tote. She would just have to dispose of it later, when no one was around. Opening the stall door, Mia stepped out.

Skylar and Riley were standing at the sink, touching up their already flawless makeup. The key to being one of Ivy's friends was to be beautiful without being too beautiful. No one was allowed to outshine Ivy Bliss.

That had never been a problem for Mia. She barely had enough time in the morning to shower and brush her teeth. Maybe apply a little eyeliner. A slash of neutral lipstick. Tucking her hair behind her ears, she'd don her uniform of black skinny pants and some sort of blouse. Her only jewelry was a pair of diamond studs she got for her sixteenth birthday.

"What are you two doing here?" Mia asked as she exited the stall. She stepped to the sink to wash her hands, avoiding eye contact with either of Ivy's friends.

"We're here to spend the day with Ivy and help her get ready for the AMAs."

"She doesn't need your help." Mia didn't make any effort to hide her impatience and didn't care if she sounded rude. She'd had enough of these two. "Ivy has a team of professionals to get her ready."

Skylar pouted. "She wants us."

"She told us to come," Riley echoed.

Mia wasn't sure what to believe, but didn't get a chance to argue further because the bathroom door opened and Ivy walked in. She glanced from her two friends to Mia and frowned.

"What are you doing in here?" she demanded. "I've been looking for you all over."

"I was explaining to these two that you don't need them around today."

Ivy pouted. "I invited them."

"You need to focus on tonight." Mia eyed Skylar. "They will just distract you. Come on. Jennifer is going to be at the house in an hour for your massage and Yvonne and her team are coming by at eleven."

"In a second." Ivy headed toward one of the stalls. "Can you go get the car? My feet are killing me in these shoes and I don't feel like walking all the way out to the parking lot."

"Fine."

Mia didn't want to argue with her sister. She was too excited about her own plans for later that day. Nate had pulled out all the stops to make her AMA experience special. He'd arranged for her to have a hotel suite where he was staying, and his stylist would be there at two o'clock with a designer dress and all the trappings to get Mia award-ceremony ready.

Ten minutes later, after Mia had fetched the car and picked up her sister, they were heading back to Ivy's house. "How did the interview go?"

"It went okay. Didn't you stay to watch?"

"I had a quick errand to run."

Ivy yawned. "I'm dead. Can you stop and get me my usual with three shots? I need a pick-me-up."

"Sure." Mia resisted the urge to talk her sister out of such a massive caffeine hit. If Ivy was ever going to start taking care of herself, Mia would have to stop making all her decisions for her.

She drove to Ivy's favorite coffee shop near her house, parked and grabbed her wallet out of her tote. "Anything else?"

"One of those scones with the raspberry."

"The white chocolate one?"

Ivy nodded and Mia headed off. Thanks to the long line, it took her fifteen minutes to get back to her sister.

"They didn't have any of the white chocolate so I got you one with orange and cranberry." Mia set the coffee cup in the drink holder and held out the bag containing the pastry.

Ivy took it without looking up from her phone. She was idly scrolling through pictures and acted as if Mia hadn't spoken. The change of mood wasn't unexpected. Ivy hated being kept waiting for anything.

And then as they pulled up in front of the house,

Ivy spoke. "I'm going to get Hunter to produce my album."

"What?" Mia glanced at her sister in confusion. "Are you sure that's a good idea? I mean, he's had some success, but at the same time he's still pretty new to that side of the business. And the label is expecting Nate to be involved."

"I don't like the direction Nate is taking my album. I want to do things my way."

Often when Mia dealt with Ivy she felt as if she stood between a rock and a hard place. Part of her job was to keep Ivy happy. The other part was more difficult. She needed to keep her sister's career on a strong trajectory. That meant keeping the label happy.

"Of course you do. But at the same time you have to consider the best for your career."

"You don't think I know what's best for my career?"

"Sure. Of course." Mia decided retreat was the best option.

Ivy got out of the car, and once she was in the house, headed straight to her room without saying another word. After checking in with the housekeeper, Clara, Mia grabbed her overnight bag and left. She was too excited about her own plans to stick around and let Ivy's drama spoil the rest of her day.

Mia had booked a spa appointment for herself as a special treat. She'd planned for a facial, pedicure and manicure to get her in the perfect mood for the festive event. It was rare for her to get so much un-interrupted time to herself, and several hours later she felt both relaxed and refreshed as she headed to the suite Nate had booked and put herself into his stylist Patricia's capable hands.

Although Mia had watched Ivy get ready for dozens of award shows and thought she knew what to expect, when she saw her dress for the first time she nearly started to cry.

"That's the most beautiful thing I've ever seen."

Patricia smiled at her and Mia wondered what she must be thinking of this silly girl Nate had asked her to dress for the event.

"I'm glad you like it. When Nate described you to me, I knew immediately this dress would be perfect for you. There's so much going on with the wild-flower print that I think we should keep your styling simple."

Patricia directed the hairdresser to sweep her hair back into a sleek bun. A smoky eye shadow and rose lipstick accentuated Mia's features. By the time they were done even Mia believed she looked presentable enough for the red carpet. Not that she would be walking with Nate. She'd put her foot down on that score. He had his bandmates to speak for him. Her appearance at his side would only lead the media to ask questions.

"You look fantastic," Patricia said as Mia finished slipping into sparkling sandals and straightened so the stylist could assess her total look. "I know several stars who would kill to have that cleavage."

Mia's fingers coasted over her still-flat belly as she stared at herself in the mirror. The neckline of the gown plunged to her waist, yet somehow managed to look elegant rather than sexy. Mia guessed it was due to the delicate sprays of sequin-accented wild-flowers that covered the skirt and halter-style top.

"I'm pretty sure I'll never wear anything so beautiful again." The dress fit as if it had been made for her and had required only a few minor alterations. "What time does it turn into fairy dust?"

Patricia laughed. "So I'm your fairy godmother?"

"You had to work some serious magic to get me looking this good."

"You underestimate how beautiful you are. I suppose it's hard to feel pretty when you're constantly comparing yourself to Ivy Bliss."

"I don't compare myself," Mia said without a hint of bitterness. "Everyone else does that for me."

"I know one person who doesn't. Nate. You are his star."

Mia's cheeks heated at Patricia's knowing grin. Because she doubted the stylist would believe anything she had to say to the contrary, she said nothing at all.

Twenty minutes later she was in a car heading for the venue. She'd followed Ivy's day on social media and saw that her sister was excited about her look for that evening. She'd teased bits of the dress all day for her fans. It was a toss-up which Ivy loved more, fashion or performing. She talked all the time about starting her own clothing line and sketched ideas in her free time.

Determined to bridge the gap developing between her and Ivy, Mia texted her twin to ask if she liked her gown, but received no reply.

She decided to go early in order to slip past the media while they were still in setup mode. Her decision turned out to be sound, but she was surprised at how many people wanted to talk to her. Unlike the commotion caused when Ivy and other big stars walked the carpet, Mia was able to take her time with several of the reporters she knew. If they were surprised to find her walking the red carpet on her own, they made no mention of it.

Once she was inside the theater, several producers Ivy had worked with in the past approached her to chat. Apparently word had gone around that Mia had been working with Nate these last few weeks. Most everyone wanted to know if she was writing as well as producing. She kept her answers vague, but by the time she reached her seat, she felt as if she belonged.

It was a heady sensation, but one she reined in almost immediately. So what if she belonged? It wasn't as if she was free to pursue her dreams. Not as long as Ivy needed her. Yet Nate's question continued to plague her. How long was she planning to keep her life on hold so she could watch over her sister? Ivy was a grown woman, no longer a fragile seventeen-year-old girl getting a taste of stardom for the first time.

Besides, in seven months, Mia's priorities would undergo a massive change. She fanned her finger over her stomach. Pregnant. A chill raced through her at the thought of how everyone around her would react to that news. She imagined her parents would be disappointed in her for not being married. Despite having a daughter who pranced around half-naked onstage, they were conservative when it came to family values. Mia was afraid of how Ivy would react. She hoped her twin would be happy for her, but Ivy rarely liked it when good things happened to Mia.

And how would Nate react? What was going on between them was fun and exciting, but it was also new and undefined. They'd known each other only a few months and weren't exactly dating. To go from lovers to parents without all the stuff in between would be a huge leap. But there wasn't any question in Mia's mind that it was one she was ready to make. So when did she tell Nate?

Tonight was too soon. When Ivy's album was done? Mia shook her head. At the rate things were going, with her sister lobbying to switch producers from Nate to Hunter, getting the recording finished by the end of November wasn't going to happen.

Tomorrow they were heading back to Las Vegas. Thursday was Thanksgiving and she and Nate had talked about spending the day together, cooking a special dinner for Trent, Savannah, Melody and hopefully Kyle. She would tell Nate then.

Blinded by the flash of dozens of cameras, Nate squelched his irritation as he walked the AMAs' red carpet with the other members of Free Fall. Although he'd convinced Mia to accompany him to the event, he'd been unable to persuade her to walk beside him past the gauntlet of paparazzi and press. Nor had he caught a glimpse of her to see how Patricia had styled her. The curiosity was killing him.

Behind them Ivy posed and vamped for the cameras. Tonight she'd abandoned her signature high ponytail for a sleek side bun that complemented her romantic red ball gown with its tiers of gauzy layers. The halter top bared her back and shoulders, but offered full frontal coverage. Fabric roses circled the high neck and waist. The deep scarlet tint showed off her light olive skin and caught every eye.

Nate put on his easy grin and posed with his bandmates. They took selfies and signed autographs for their fans. It was great to step away from his role as front man and let the other guys answer the interviewers' questions. All the while his mind was on what awaited him at the end of the red carpet.

After what felt like a ridiculous amount of time, but was only about a half an hour, they entered the theater and headed to their seats. He saw a woman sitting in one of the seats assigned to Free Fall, her brown hair knotted at the nape of her neck. All Nate's tension fell away as he reached the row and realized it was Mia. While his heart thundered in his ears, he suddenly realized he'd half expected her not to show.

She stared straight ahead with fixed concentration, as if by holding herself perfectly still no one would notice her. She was completely mistaken. For starters, she was wearing the exact opposite of Ivy's gown. This dress boasted a deep V that bared Mia from throat to waist, yet somehow managed to look elegant rather than overly sexy. Nate realized it was the gown's off-white background and the sprays of vivid printed flowers with their hints of sparkle that gave the dress a feminine vibe.

Her expression softened as she saw him approach. Nate's pulse hitched at the relief in her eyes. Or maybe it was just how perfect she looked. And smelled. This last he noted as he sat beside her and brushed her cheek with his lips.

"You look gorgeous," he signed, not trusting his voice. Although he'd been cleared by Dr. Hansen to talk a little, he'd grown accustomed to communicating with her in ASL.

"You look pretty great yourself." She glanced past him at his other bandmates and gave them all a sweet smile. "Are you guys nervous?"

"Nah." Mike, their keyboard player, had his arm wrapped around his smiling wife.

Their base player, Dan, was riding solo tonight.

His very pregnant wife had opted to cheer from home. "Hell, yeah."

"Sort of." This last came from their drummer, Brent, who had a stunning blonde in a sequined mini on his arm.

Mia laughed, the sound light and musical. "I would think you guys are old pros at this. How many Grammys have you won?"

Nate took his seat as he listened to Mia banter with his bandmates. Sitting beside her, he was a little surprised at his light-headedness. The weight he'd been carrying all afternoon lifted. He took her hand, lacing their fingers together, and brought it to his lips.

The theater was filling with musicians. They were fifteen minutes away from the start of the show. Beside Nate, Mia was a bundle of restless energy.

"Did you see Ivy?" she asked.

"She was behind us on the red carpet."

"How did she look?"

"Beautiful as always. She was wearing a red dress."

Mia nodded. "I saw bits of it on Instagram. The style is a departure for her and I think she was both excited and a little nervous about wearing it."

Nate was slightly surprised she'd let him tuck her arm through his. Then he realized, given the way she was looking around at all the celebrities, she probably hadn't even noticed the intimacy between them.

The same couldn't be said for him. He was hyperaware of every little thing about her, from her muted squeal when Taylor Swift walked past to her soft gasp when Luke Bryan winked at her. Given how often she must have seen these people at other award shows, her starstruck behavior amused him. She was like a kid at Disneyland for the first time.

"It's different sitting in the audience among them," she explained when she caught him grinning at her. "I don't have to be professional."

By professional he sensed what she meant was invisible. She'd learned how to bottle up all her emotions, good and bad. He'd realized this when they first met on tour. They'd hung out for almost three weeks before he realized she liked him the way he liked her.

Excitement hummed in her slim body. "I don't think I could ever get used to this."

"They're all just people, like me and you."

"You're not just people. You're Nate Tucker." She stated his name as if that explained everything.

"I'm just a guy."

She shook her head as if he could never understand. Her voice was soft as she spoke. "I still have a hard time believing you ever noticed me."

Conscious of their surroundings, he resisted the urge to sweep her into his arms and kiss her soft lips. *"Let's go find a quiet corner and I'll notice you plenty."*

Even now after everything they'd shared, she still blushed when he stared at her intently. That she'd somehow maintained such innocence while immersed in show business craziness continued to enthrall him.

"I'm glad you came tonight."

"Me, too." But there was a hint of hesitation in her answer.

She was still worried about Ivy. Nate was of two minds. Part of him was irritated at the hold her sister maintained over her. The other part sympathized with Mia. He knew firsthand the effect of being bullied by family. His father hadn't treated his wife and child as though they mattered to him. On a good day he'd settled in front of the television with a whiskey and ignored them. On a bad day he'd led with his fists.

Music began to play, signaling that the show was getting under way. Mia relaxed and snuggled a bit closer. Had she been worried that her sister might stop by and make a scene? What was it going to take for Mia to get out from beneath Ivy's thumb?

It was nice for a change to not have to worry about performing. The only time he needed to leave Mia alone was a little over an hour and a half into the program, when Free Fall presented the award for Favorite Male Country Artist. He stood to the side while Dan and Mike took turns reading off the nominees. While the winner thanked family and fans, Nate shared a smile with Mia. She looked so perfect sitting there, her eyes bright, her gaze all for him as she waited for him to come back to her.

All of a sudden he couldn't wait for the show to be over so he could take her to the after-party and spend some time with her in his arms on the dance floor. Since she was officially his date, Mia couldn't possibly use her sister's presence as an excuse to keep him at bay the way she'd done on the tour.

But he'd underestimated Ivy.

When the pop star stepped onstage to perform, something was definitely off with her. Nate doubted most people would notice, but he'd watched her rehearse and perform for weeks while on tour. She was a beat behind the music and she was walking through her complicated choreography. Mia sat forward in her chair, her expression tightening with concern.

"What's wrong with her?"

Mia shook her head, but he knew her well enough to know when she wasn't telling the truth.

"Is she drunk?"

Mia's gaze was glued to Ivy. Nate wasn't sure if she'd even noticed his questions, until she shook her head again after a minute.

"Maybe high." Mia set her fingertips against her mouth and blinked rapidly. The bright glint in her eyes was from tears. "I need to get backstage and be there for her."

"Then we'll both go." He wasn't letting Mia run off without him. She might never come back.

"You can't leave in the middle of the ceremony."

But she could. It was her way of highlighting the difference in their status. She was a lowly, anonymous assistant, while he was a celebrity. Nate was getting tired of it.

"Contact your dad. He's her manager. Let him deal with her."

Mia bit the inside of her lip, looking concerned at his insistence. "I'll call him when I get backstage."

Nate cursed long and viciously in his head. Leave it to Ivy to upset her sister just when Mia was having fun. Nate reached for her hand, but Mia pulled it out of reach before he made contact.

"I'll be back in a little while."

Then, as the performance ended and the crowd politely applauded, Mia slipped away. And Nate wondered if he'd see her again before the evening was over.

Nine

It was a little after midnight when Nate returned to his hotel suite without his date for the evening. He wasn't surprised that Mia hadn't reappeared after heading backstage to check on her sister. At least she hadn't left him hanging. She'd sent him several texts as she assessed the situation and waited for her father to show up and take charge of Ivy.

Now, his cell phone pinged and his screen lit up with a text.

I'm back at the hotel. Sorry about what happened tonight.

The tightness in his chest eased as he texted her back, letting her know that he was also at the hotel and asking her to come to his suite. It was time he and Mia had a serious conversation about what was going on between them and where he saw their relationship going. He needed to know where she stood.

A soft knock sounded on his door. When he opened it, Mia stood in the hallway holding a pint of his favorite ice cream and two spoons.

"What's that for?"

"Girls always eat ice cream after a big disappointment."

He wondered which disappointment she referred to: the fact that Free Fall didn't win their category or that her sister had ruined his evening.

"I'm not a girl. And I don't care that we lost." He plucked the ice cream from her hand and gestured her in.

"I am a girl and the ice cream is for me. I just thought I'd share." She swiped at the container, but he moved beyond her reach.

He set the ice cream on the coffee table and sat down on the couch. *"It's my favorite. And what do you have to be bummed about?"*

"You're mad at me."

"I'm not."

"Liar." She followed him and sat down cross-legged, facing him. "I'm sorry I ruined our night."

"You didn't. Your sister did."

"I shouldn't have left you."

In five minutes she'd managed to dispel his annoyance and arouse his sympathy. Here he'd been feeling sorry for himself, and she was the one who'd had to disrupt her evening to take care of Ivy.

"How come you didn't tell me your sister has a drug problem?"

The question had been burning up his thoughts since he'd realized what's going on.

"She doesn't have a problem."

Mia's evasion annoyed him. It wasn't just that she was keeping a whopping huge secret from him. Ivy's career was something Nate and Trent were investing time and money in. If there was a problem, they needed to know.

"You don't think I can see what's going on? You forget, I've been there."

Mia wouldn't meet his gaze. "I know, but you got clean and Ivy can, too."

"Who knows about this?"

"Just my immediate family."

"How long has this been going on?"

"It started when she had plastic surgery at seventeen. She got hooked on the painkillers. She was on Broadway at the time and I was finishing up my senior year of high school in LA. No one knows this but my parents and me, but she almost died after overdosing." Mia looked miserable. "That's when it was decided I should become her assistant so I could keep an eye on her."

"But it's been eight years." At least this explained Mia's dedication to her sister. *"How long is everyone expecting you to sacrifice your life for Ivy?"*

She didn't answer his question. "She doesn't always make good choices. I've been worried about her spending so much time with Riley and Skylar. They are far more likely to drag her into trouble than they are to keep her out of it."

"How bad are things with her?"

"She's been mostly clean since what happened in New York."

"Mostly?"

Mia winced. "Except for a setback a couple years ago."

"She seemed fine on the tour."

"She was. It's the album. She's really struggling. But I don't know what happened tonight. Usually she loves performing."

Nate had a pretty good idea. *"It's because you're here with me. Your sister loves to spoil things for you."*

"That's not true." But she didn't sound or look convincing.

When Mia offered nothing else, he asked another question. *"Does your father know what's going on?"*

"Before. But not this time around."

"You should tell him. He's her father." Nate thought that Javier needed to act like her father for a change and put his manager role on the back burner. "This could ruin more than just her career."

Mia dropped her gaze to her hands. Misery radiated from her. The tour had offered Nate plenty of chances to observe the family dynamic and he sensed more at work here that Mia wasn't saying.

"What?"

"They'll blame me." She leaned forward and dug her spoon into the ice cream. "That's not true. I don't mean that." But it was obvious that was exactly what worried her. "It's just that I'm supposed to keep an eye on her. And I've been distracted." The sly smile she shot him wobbled at the edges.

His heart broke. *"Why do you let them do that to you?"*

"Because she's my sister and I'm…"

"Responsible for her?"

He'd never had a brother or sister and didn't understand the connection these two had. To make matters worse, Ivy and Mia were twins. Granted, they were fraternal rather than identical twins, but still, sharing a womb with someone for nine months must take the bond to a whole different level.

"Where does it end?" Hopelessness overwhelmed him as he suddenly realized his plan to disengage Mia from her sister had been doomed from the start. *"When do you get to live your life?"*

"I don't know."

His mother had stayed with a bully too long and she'd ended up beaten and bruised on too many occasions. Mia wore her wounds on the inside.

On the other hand, he wasn't sure if Mia was ready to leave her situation. Shucking off her family's expectations couldn't be easy. He'd seen firsthand the pressure Javier exerted on both his daughters.

"Have you asked yourself what you owe her?"

"I know you don't think I owe her anything," Mia said. "Maybe I don't. I just know if I leave and something happens to her again, I would never be able to forgive myself."

That sort of emotional blackmail was nearly impossible to walk away from. Nate wished he could somehow make her understand what they were doing to her. Or maybe she did. Maybe the way she coped was to pretend it didn't bother her.

More than anything Nate wanted to protect her from herself. He'd be her champion if she'd let him. But he couldn't force her to get out of the bad situation she found herself in. Unlike when he'd stepped between his parents and wrestled the knife away from his father, the danger to Mia wasn't tangible. But that didn't make it any less dire.

"How much longer can you keep it up? Following Ivy around. Keeping her out of trouble. Catering to her every whim. When do you get to live your life?"

He'd posed this same question several times on tour. Each time Mia had given him the same answer.

"It's what I need to do right now. Once Ivy's new album drops and it's a sensation, I'll have more options." Her eyes pleaded with him to understand. "I promised my parents to watch out for her. She doesn't take good care of herself. That leads to people taking advantage of her. Like Riley and Skylar are doing right now."

"You say you're going to leave after this album launches, but what if she needs you more than ever?"

That Mia didn't answer immediately told him a lot.

"You know I'm in your corner, right?"

"I do." But she didn't look at him.

For a moment he felt as if she didn't want him to be in her corner. As if having him on her side created a whole new set of problems for her. How was that possible?

"Where does this leave us?"

"I just need some time to sort things out."

"How much time?" He had to head back to Las Vegas tomorrow, but hated the idea of leaving her behind in LA.

"My parents are sitting down with Ivy tomorrow. I'll know more then."

"Are you coming back to Las Vegas?"

"I promised I'd help with Thanksgiving dinner." She gave him a wan smile. "We can talk then."

The morning after the AMAs, Mia drove Nate to a checkup with Dr. Hanson and then to the airport. As delighted as she'd been to hear that Nate's progress was good and he was able to start speaking again, she would miss being his voice. That he'd needed her to translate for him was a great excuse for why she was spending so much time with him.

Now, she'd have to come clean about their relationship and face Ivy's displeasure.

When Mia got to her sister's house, she saw their
mom's car parked in the driveway. Mia approached
the front door with a sick feeling in her stomach.
Her mother stood in the foyer as Mia entered the
house. As Ivy's career had taken off, Sharon Navarro had changed from an average housewife and
mother who'd homeschooled her three daughters and
shopped discount stores for her clothes to a designer-
label-wearing middle-aged woman with large dia-
monds at her ears and on her fingers. Despite what
must have been a harrowing night worrying about
Ivy, she looked as if she was ready for lunch at a
fancy restaurant.

In contrast, Mia felt disheveled and gritty despite the shower she'd shared with Nate that morning. "What are you doing here?" she asked, hoping
nothing worse had happened to her sister overnight.
"Is Ivy okay?"

"She's fine. Where have you been?"

"At the hotel. I told Dad last night where I was
going. I needed to return the dress."

"And you stayed?"

Although they'd spent the night together, talking
and making love until dawn, she couldn't help but
feel as if Nate had put a wall up between them. He
wanted her to leave Ivy and be with him. Mia thought
that's what she wanted, too. So why couldn't she just
walk away? Because Ivy needed her? How long was

she going to use that as an excuse? Especially now that she was pregnant.

"I knew Dad was here. Ivy didn't need us both." Mia's tone contained a touch of belligerence. "I had a whole night planned." To her own surprise, she sounded like Ivy, petulant and frustrated.

"Do you mean to tell me you went to the after-parties after dropping your sister off here?" Mia's mother looked appalled.

"No, of course not. I just wanted to point out that I had my own plans for the evening that didn't involve my sister getting high and making a fool of herself on live television."

"Mia," her mother admonished. "Your sister works so hard and is under such pressure."

Fury rushed through Mia's body as she thought of her high hopes for last evening. It was supposed to her magical night. Her chance to appear in public with Nate and behave like a couple. To dance and mingle and have fun while not giving her sister a single thought.

"She spoils everything," Mia countered.

"She supports all of us."

"Well, maybe I'm tired of being supported by her. Maybe it's time I started supporting myself."

When had her level of resentment risen so high? How had she not noticed that each day of acting as her sister's assistant grew harder than the one before? Nate's constant pointing out how badly Ivy treated her didn't help.

Mia's mother retreated a half step beneath the rush of her daughter's emotional tirade. "You can't turn your back on her sister. She isn't strong enough to do this on her own."

"I'm not turning my back on her." All the energy drained from her. No matter what she said or did, Mia was never going to win this battle. It all came down to guilt. Responsibility. "She's my sister and I love her. But my life revolves around her and I want a little something for myself."

"You mean your songwriting," Mia's mother said. "I'll speak to your father. Maybe there's room on Ivy's next album for a few of your songs. And this time you should get the credit."

"That's not what I mean." But Mia could tell her mother wasn't listening.

Her fingers shifted to her abdomen and the child that lay there. Now wasn't the time to get into this with her mom. She needed to talk to Nate first.

But right now, Mia needed some sleep. The past twenty-four hours had been a roller coaster of highs and lows, all of which had taken every ounce of Mia's energy.

"Can we talk about this later?" she said. "I'm exhausted. Are you going to stick around for a while?"

"No. I have a meeting at the foundation."

Sharon Navarro ran the Ivy Bliss Foundation, a program that promoted hearing health and helped low-income children with hearing impairments. It was a charity near and dear to her heart because of her eldest daughter's hearing loss at age two.

"Where is Dad?"

"Your father's meeting with Trent Caldwell about Ivy's album. It looks as if she's going to finish recording it with Hunter Graves." Mia's mother picked up her purse. "He'll come by afterward."

"Then I guess it's just me keeping an eye on her." Again.

"I don't understand what has gotten into you lately. You used to be happy for your sister's success."

"I still am. But she's become such a different person. There are times when I don't recognize her anymore."

"She's a star," Mia's mother said, as if that explained everything.

Overwhelmed by defeat, Mia watched her mother depart before shuffling toward her bedroom. She shut the door behind her and glanced around the space. Besides the clothes in the closet, barely anything in the room belonged to her. Mia dropped her overnight bag on the floor and flung herself on her bed, where she lay on her back, staring at the ceiling. Her eyes were dry despite the lump in her throat.

She didn't remember ever feeling so alone. And yet, what about her situation had changed? Acting as her sister's full-time personal assistant and keeper had kept Mia from forming lasting friendships, and interfered with every man she'd ever tried to date.

Except now, Mia had been given a glimpse of what her life could be. A career as a music producer. Friendships with Melody, Trent and Savannah. A relationship with Nate. Motherhood.

Mia closed her eyes. Ready or not, everything was going to change.

Nate was surprised when the person picking him up at the Las Vegas airport was Kyle and not Melody. As he slid into the passenger seat of Kyle's bright blue BMW convertible, he glanced at his business partner and thought he looked as exhausted and miserable as Nate felt.

"I didn't expect to see you," Nate said.

"Melody asked if I could get you. Seems she had a small window to get Hunter's input on her album—" Kyle's eyes widened. "Hey, you're talking again."

"My doctor gave me the go-ahead to start using my voice, but I'm not supposed to overdo it. So you and Melody are finally talking?"

"If by talking you mean she sent me a text saying she was stuck at the studio and would I pick you up, then yeah."

Nate winced at the other man's bitterness. "You two have got to sit down and chat. Why don't you come for Thanksgiving." Nate had extended the invitation to Kyle once already and been turned down. This time, he decided to push harder.

"I don't want to spoil the day for you guys."

"You won't." The only thing that could spoil the

day for Nate was if Mia found a reason not to show. "The longer you and Melody keep up whatever it is you're doing, the harder it's going to be to reconcile."

"What if we're not meant to be together?"

Kyle's question hit at the heart of what Nate himself had been grappling with these last few weeks. And after last night, he was more convinced than ever that when the time came, Mia was going to bolt the same way she had that last morning in Sydney.

And what then? What was he planning to do without her? He couldn't bear to think about it.

"You and Melody love each other," Nate said. And in less than six months they were going to become parents, whether either of them was prepared or not. "You'll find a way to work it out. Just remember why you fell for her in the first place."

"But I've really messed up. I pretty much accused her of cheating on me with Hunter."

Nate could appreciate his friend's predicament. Kyle was a well-known player. Before realizing he was in love with Melody, he'd dated lots of women and committed to none of them.

"Have you asked yourself why?"

"Many times. It's the way Melody and I got together. She was trying to make Hunter jealous. I keep thinking maybe she picked the wrong guy."

Nate didn't think this was the heart of Kyle's troubles. It seemed more likely that he was afraid to give himself over to the intense feelings Melody aroused in him. Nate got it. Falling in love was a big, scary deal. As he was discovering.

"You don't really believe that?"

"That picture of them together in New York. She looked so happy with him. It's been months and months since she's been like that with me..." Kyle's voice trailed off and silence reigned in the car for a while. "And now he's here and working at your studio," he finally added. "I'm sure she's spending tons of time with him. He's going to win her back," Kyle grumbled. "If he hasn't already."

"So that's it then?" Nate's tone was harsh. He wanted Kyle to man up and fight for the woman he loved. "You're giving up?"

"I didn't say that."

"It sure as hell sounds like it."

Kyle opened his mouth but no words came out. Nate would love it if the only problem between him and Mia was a stupid misunderstanding about a photo of her with an ex-boyfriend.

"You're both acting like a couple of idiots," Nate declared. "Things between you might have moved fast, but that's no reason to freak out. Stop being so dense. Tell her you love her and make her believe it."

For a long time Kyle didn't say anything. Then, as he turned the car onto Nate's street, he said, "Thanksgiving, huh? What time should I be there?"

"Dinner's at five, but you're welcome at any time. Trent and Dylan are coming early for the Vikings-

Lions game. Savannah and Melody plan on coming midafternoon."

"Can I bring anything?"

Nate grinned. "Just your best behavior. Mia and I will provide the rest."

Twenty minutes later, after switching to his own car at home, Nate was pulling into the studio parking lot. The receptionist greeted him with a wave when he went inside. He popped into a couple different control booths to see how things were going. He found Melody on the couch in studio C with Hunter at the boards.

When she spotted him, Melody jumped up and rushed across the room to throw her arms around his neck.

"Thanks for sending Kyle to pick me up."

"Sorry about the switch, but Hunter had a free hour to help me out. Hey, you got your voice back." Melody beamed at him. "But you shouldn't overdo it."

"I won't." Nate turned to Hunter. "How's it going with her album?"

"She's got a lot of great songs here. We'll just have to whittle it down." The look he gave Melody sent a wave of apprehension through Nate. "It might take a while."

Maybe Kyle had reason to be concerned, after all. Not because Melody was falling for her ex-boyfriend, but because Hunter had a very possessive look in his eye when he gazed at her. As if he might be planning to work damned hard to win her back.

"Not too long, I hope," Nate said. "I'd like to have it ready to go by the beginning of next year."

"I'll put all my energy into making that happen." Hunter shot Melody a fond look. "But now I've got to get going. Dinner later?"

"Ah, sure."

"I'll pick you up at six."

When Hunter left the control booth, Nate turned on Melody. "What the hell is going on between you two?"

"Nothing. We're just friends."

"And Kyle?"

Melody toyed with her phone. "Kyle and I need some space."

"That's the last thing you need. Have you forgotten that you two are going to be parents? When do you plan to tell him about the baby?" Nate saw the excuses gathering in her eyes and shook his head. "I've invited him for Thanksgiving. You'll be surrounded by family. We'll all be there to support you. Plan on telling him then."

"But that's only three days away."

"The sooner the better."

"So tell me what happened with Ivy at the AMAs last night. She looked out of it."

"Apparently she's been addicted to painkillers on and off for the last eight years and recently suffered

a relapse. Mia stayed behind in LA while they figure out the best way to handle things."

"Trent is meeting with Javier today." Melody's
features wore a worried expression. "Do you think
he'll postpone her album?"

"The way things have been going, it might be a
good idea to push it out until later next year. She
needs to focus on getting clean again." Nate thought
about his plunge down the rabbit hole of drug and
alcohol abuse and didn't envy Ivy for what she had
to look forward to. "I'm off to get some work done."
He leaned over and kissed Melody on the forehead.
"Give what I said about you and Kyle some thought
before you head off to dinner with Hunter tonight,
okay?"

Melody nodded and Nate left to make some music
and figure out what he was going to do about Mia
next.

Early Tuesday afternoon, Mia was in her bedroom at Ivy's LA house, sorting through recipes and
planning the shopping list for her Thanksgiving dinner with Nate and his friends when the door burst
open and Skylar plunged into the room with Riley
on her heels.

Since she'd returned from dropping Nate at the
airport the day before, Mia had either been holed up
in her room to escape the thick tension filling the
house, or popping in every couple hours to check
on Ivy. So far, her sister hadn't shown much inter-

est in anything besides binge watching *Pretty Little Liars* on Hulu.

"You bitch!" Skylar shrieked, her wild eyes fixed on Mia.

"What?" Mia stared at her dumbfounded, unsure what Skylar and Riley were doing in Ivy's house, much less Mia's room.

Ivy must have let them in. Why couldn't she understand that she was supposed to cut all ties with these two? They were the ones who'd been supplying her with the prescription drugs. Mia jumped off her bed as Skylar advanced toward her.

"You have some nerve," Ivy's friend said in a threatening tone.

Mia glanced from Skylar to Riley. "You need to leave. Now."

"We're not going anywhere," Riley piped up. "We know it was you."

Mia shook her head. "It's not just me. My father wants you to stay away from Ivy, too." But she could tell the two women weren't listening to her.

"Haven't you sponged off your sister long enough?"

These two were the most clueless women on the planet. "Sponged? Do you have any idea what I do for Ivy?"

"Well, you don't write her music. That's for sure."

Skylar's words made Mia go cold. Everyone who knew the truth behind Ivy's songwriting worked awfully hard to keep it hidden. Neither one of these two was trustworthy enough to be told such a damaging secret.

"Of course not," Mia said calmly, while her heart thundered.

"Then why did you tell the media that Ivy didn't write any of her songs?"

"I didn't." Mia was besieged by panic. Such a disclosure would devastate Ivy. "I wouldn't do that."

"Sure you would," Riley said.

Skylar nodded. "You resent her."

"I don't." But she could hear the lie in her voice.

She did resent Ivy, but not for the reasons these two thought. Mia didn't care that Ivy had been gifted with all the looks and talent. Up until the last few years, when Ivy had started behaving more and more like a diva, Mia had been happy to be her assistant and do whatever she could to bolster her twin's career.

"Sure you do." Riley exchanged a look with Skylar. "You have a thing for Nate."

"We all noticed."

"But he doesn't know you're alive. He wants Ivy. So you decided to discredit her by lying to the media and saying you're the one who writes her music."

It was on the tip of Mia's tongue to argue that she did write all Ivy's music, but too many years of living with that secret kept her silent now. "I need to talk to Ivy."

Mia started toward Ivy's bedroom, but Riley stepped in her way.

"She doesn't want to talk to you."

Irritation flooded Mia, loosening her tongue. "If you want to talk about people who sponge off my sister, look in the mirror." Imbued with strength she didn't know she possessed, Mia pushed past Riley and headed toward her sister's bedroom. She had to explain.

Ivy was standing by the open sliding glass door that led onto the pool deck, Mia's song journal in her hand. Mia stopped halfway into the room as Ivy turned her tear-streaked face in her direction.

"I didn't tell anyone about the songwriting," Mia said, her voice clogged with emotion. "I swear."

"Not even Nate?"

"He figured it out all on his own." Mia advanced toward her sister, but Ivy went outside, maintaining ten feet between them.

"You're such a liar." Ivy held out the notebook. "I read this. It's all about him."

Mia's song journal was more than just a place for her to jot down music and lyrics. She also used it as a diary, and although she'd never used Nate's name, many of the entries had described incidents that made it pretty clear who she was talking about.

"I'll bet you couldn't wait to tell him," Ivy continued. "You probably thought he'd be into you if he thought you were a songwriter."

"I swear I didn't tell him." But in her heart, she knew she'd wanted him to figure it out. And maybe she'd helped that along. "It was just that I wrote songs with Melody on the tour and you never showed any signs that you wrote, too. He got suspicious."

"What other bad things have you been telling Nate about me?"

"I haven't said anything."

Ivy gave a bitter laugh. "I see the way you moon over him. He's never going to be interested in you."

"Why do you care how I feel about Nate?"

"I don't." But it was obvious that she was bothered. "I just hate to see you make a fool of yourself over someone who is so out of your league."

"Nate doesn't see himself that way." The instant the words were past her lips, Mia wished them back.

"He should."

Without warning, Ivy launched Mia's song journal through the air in the direction of the pool. Mia watched in horror as hundreds of hours' worth of angst and love hit the water with a splat and began to sink.

"My journal." An anguished cry broke from her as she rushed forward. She stood at the edge of the pool with her hands over her mouth, unable to believe her sister could have done something so cruel. "What the hell, Ivy?"

Her twin glared at her. "Now there's no proof who wrote those songs."

"You forget that I have years' worth of those journals. Every one of them proves you've been taking credit for my songs. Are you planning on destroying those, as well?"

"Yes."

"Why are you doing this? All we have to do is release a press statement that confirms you write your own songs."

"Why did you have to ruin everything?" Ivy demanded.

"I didn't do anything."

"It's all your fault. Every bit of it." Tears streamed down Ivy's cheeks. "I can't look at you anymore."

"Ivy, why don't you calm down and let's talk about this." Her sister's behavior was scaring Mia. She started to put her hands on Ivy's arms in an effort to connect with her, but her twin threw her off and backed up.

"There's no need to talk. I hate you. I want you out of this house and out of my life. I'm sick of having you telling me what to do and where to go."

"I only do that because I'm your assistant." Mia's frustration was continuing to build; she was at her breaking point. "It's my job to keep you on schedule."

"Well, I'm sick of it. I don't need you."

"What are you saying?"

"I'm saying I don't want you around anymore. Get the hell out of my house."

Ten

Tuesday night after a lonely dinner by himself, Nate sat in his living room with his guitar for company and came to terms with just how miserable he was being a bachelor. He was sick of coming home to an empty house and sleeping alone in his big bed. Sexy Skyping with Mia last night had been more frustrating than fun. He needed her here and now. Tomorrow couldn't come soon enough.

His phone buzzed. Hoping it was Mia calling, Nate reached for it. "Hey, Trent."

His business partner got right to the point without preliminaries. "Someone leaked that Ivy doesn't write her own songs."

"What?"

"Was it you?"

"No." Nate cursed, half wishing he had done it. But Mia would never have forgiven him. "When did this happen?"

"This afternoon. I just found out."

"This afternoon…" Why hadn't Mia called to tell him? She had to know. "Have you spoken to Javier?"

"Not yet. I thought, given your connection to Mia, that we should talk about how you'd like the label to handle things."

While Nate appreciated his friend's consideration, he had absolutely no idea what would be best for Mia. "I think West Coast Records should come out saying we have no knowledge of this."

"But is that true?" Trent sounded tense and weary. "I don't have any idea what sort of unscrupulous business practices the label was engaged in with my father or brother at the helm."

Where was Mia?

Was she corralled with her family as they strategized damage control? Ivy must be near hysterical. First there was the misstep at the AMAs on Sunday. And now this. But why hadn't Mia called or texted?

"What if you make a personal statement that you had no knowledge of the situation and that you will investigate and correct whatever mistakes were made."

"That feels a little bit like we're throwing Ivy under the bus." Trent's tone was neutral, giving Nate no idea which way he was leaning. "Bottom line—do you want Mia to get credit for the songs or not?"

"Let me talk to her. Can you give me a couple hours?"

"I'm not going to rush into anything. Tomorrow morning is soon enough."

Nate hung up with Trent and dialed Mia. He wasn't surprised when he got her voice mail. After leaving a message, he began to pace. Not more than five minutes later, his doorbell rang. Expecting to find Melody on his doorstep, he was shocked to see Mia.

"I was on my way here when I got your message." She looked miserable as she stood outside his front door.

He reached for her hand and pulled her inside. "Are you okay?"

"No." Mia pressed herself against his chest and mumbled her next words into his shirt. "She thinks I did it."

"You didn't, did you?"

Mia pushed away and glared up at him. "Absolutely not."

Of course not. He wasn't even sure why he'd asked. "But now that the truth is out there, Trent and I will back you one hundred percent."

"She threw my journal in the pool. There was almost six months' worth of ideas and melodies." Her small frame shook. "And she fired me as her assistant."

Nate tightened his arms around her and buried his face in her hair. It was probably best that she couldn't see his face at the moment because the news that her sister had fired her pleased him. He knew she wouldn't agree that it was the best thing for her.

She pulled out of his arms and wiped at her eyes. "I can't believe she did that."

He drew her from the foyer and into his living room. Her expression was blank, her gaze turned inward as he settled her on the couch. Once she was tucked against his body with her head resting on his shoulder, he gave a contented sigh. Her life might be falling apart, but in the depths of her despair, she'd come to him.

"I don't know what happened," she murmured after a long, long time. "One second I was working on a shopping list for Thanksgiving dinner, the next Skylar and Riley are bursting into my room and accusing me of being the one who told the media I wrote all Ivy's songs. And when I told Ivy that I wouldn't have done that, she didn't believe me." Mia's breath came in unsteady gasps as she relayed her tale. "She was half out of her mind, saying all sorts of crazy things that made no sense."

"She'll realize it wasn't you."

"I don't think she'll ever believe that. She threw me out. I don't know what that means. I've always lived with her."

This was sounding better and better by the second. "You can move in here," he said, keeping his voice as calm and gentle as possible. Mia was vulnerable. He didn't want to spook her. "Maybe this will all work out for the best," he began. "It'll be a fresh start."

"A fresh start?" She echoed the words as if she were tasting some strange and suspicious dish. "It's not over."

"I thought you said she threw you out and fired you."

"She didn't mean it."

"What if she did?" Nate intended to capitalize on this turn of good fortune. "You could come work for me. Live in Las Vegas." *Be with me.*

It was the same offer he'd made to her in Australia. The one she'd turned down without giving it a second's consideration.

"I could." Her shoulders slumped. She shook her head. "But this isn't how I wanted things to happen."

"What did you want?" Nate couldn't stop his expression from turning grim. "Her blessing? She was never going to give you that."

"I know, but this seems so abrupt. It's like she hates me. Knowing how important my song journal is to me, she ruined it. That's six months of work. Gone."

His eyebrows went up; he couldn't help it. "You forget you have the demos you made." What he'd heard was pretty fantastic. "And you'll write plenty more songs."

She made a face at him. "You make it sound so easy." Taking him by surprise, she set her hand on his cheek and brought her lips to his in a sweet, poignant kiss. "Besides, those songs were special. They were about us. How I feel when I'm with you."

Nate's heart gave a mighty thump. For a second he lost the ability to breathe. "How do you feel?"

"Like I exist."

"You've always existed to me."

"I know."

When he'd left LA yesterday morning, he'd promised himself to keep his distance until she was ready to commit to being in a relationship with him. That vow went up in smoke as she eased closer and sifted her fingers through his hair.

He had no words to deny her and no willpower to push her away. Letting his eyes close, he absorbed her breath on his skin and the gentle sweep of her lips against his. She touched him tentatively, as if she expected rejection at any second. Even if he had the strength to push her away, he'd never be able to do it. She soothed the places inside him damaged by his father's abuse and the years he'd spent drowning in forgetfulness. Until she came along, he'd filled the gnawing emptiness first with reckless amusements, and then music.

That he couldn't hold on to her, couldn't convince her his need was greater than her sister's, had nudged him close to the dark places he'd once lost himself in. Good thing he was no longer a stupid twenty-something. He might have sought the oblivion of those earlier days in his career before he'd hit rock bottom and cleaned himself up.

"About what you said to me the other night," she said. "Nate, there's something you should know—" she began, but he shook his head, cutting her off.

"Don't talk."

If they started a conversation he wouldn't be able to take her in his arms and show her how much she meant to him. Standing up, he scooped her off the couch and headed for his bedroom.

"Are you sure?" she asked, when her feet touched the floor beside his bed.

"Very sure."

He lowered his lips to her soft neck and breathed in her clean fragrance. Her fingers coasted down the front of his shirt, unfastening buttons as they went. Anticipation coiled in his gut below where she laid her palms against his skin. He shuddered, eager to revisit the heat of her body sliding against his.

"Tonight it's just you and me." And the beginning of everything.

Mia stood in Nate's kitchen, surrounded by the leftovers from their Thanksgiving dinner, and smiled in blissful contentment. In the family room, Nate, Kyle and Trent sat on the couch in front of the big screen television watching football. It was the third game of the day and Mia wondered if men ever grew tired of watching a bunch of beefy guys pass, run and tackle.

"What can I do to help?" Melody slipped into the kitchen and gazed at the packed countertops.

"I've got this," Mia said with a wistful smile. "But if you'd hang out and keep me company, that would be great."

"But you did all the cooking," Savannah said as she passed with her infant son in her arms. She placed the boy in his father's care and returned. "You shouldn't have to clean up, as well."

"I'm happy to do it. Today was one of the best Thanksgivings I've ever had." She pulled out plastic storage containers and began making meals that she intended to send home with everyone.

She'd made enough food for twenty people and what they hadn't finished was way more than she and Nate could eat by themselves.

"I agree," Melody said. "Last year Nate and I were on the road. Kyle and Trent went to Miami." She paused and glanced at Savannah. "Did Rafe make you spend the holiday with Siggy?"

"Unfortunately." Savannah shuddered.

Mia remembered hearing how Melody and Trent's father was a terrible bully who treated Trent like the black sheep of the family for no good reason.

While the two women began sharing tales of Caldwell Thanksgivings past, Mia worked methodically to restore order to the kitchen. Listening to their stories of family dysfunction eased some of her angst. Although she'd called her parents and Ivy to wish them a happy Thanksgiving, not one had picked up.

It seemed impossible that after everything she'd

done for Ivy her family could believe she was responsible for the leak. And with each hour that went by,
it seemed as though Nate was right about her being
permanently fired as Ivy's assistant.

No more demands for coffee or frivolous errands.
No more being awakened at three in the morning
when Ivy returned home from partying with her entourage, and having to fix waffles or quesadillas, depending on what her sister was in the mood for. Mia
still wasn't accustomed to the peace and quiet that
came from not being her sister's assistant any longer.

It was nice playing house with Nate. Her gaze
traveled toward the couch and lingered on the three
men. Was this what a normal Thanksgiving was like?
A house filled with great friends, good food and
football.

"Oh, I know that look," Savannah said with a
wistful sigh.

Melody chuckled. "Do you recognize it every
time you look in the mirror?"

"I recognize it from when you and Kyle first
started dating." Savannah eyed her sister-in-law.
"Don't you think it's time you two stopped playing
games and started acting like you're in love once
again?"

"Have you told him?" Mia kept her voice low.

Melody shook her head. "I was supposed to today,
but there never seemed to be an opportunity."

"We all gave you plenty of chances," Savannah
pointed out.

It had been easy to isolate the pair several times over the course of the day, but neither Melody nor Kyle seemed at ease with each other. Three times Mia had watched them engage in awkward conversation before separating. Each time her heart had ached for the pair.

With Savannah gently pressing Melody about her urgent need to talk to Kyle, Mia's own mouth went dry. She'd made a similar promise to herself about telling Nate that he was going to be a father. With all the drama surrounding Ivy, and the frantic meal preparations, it had slipped Mia's mind.

She sipped from her water bottle to alleviate her sudden cotton mouth. Anxiety made her stomach churn. As soon as she told Nate he was going to be a dad, her life would completely change.

Together they would have to decide how to move forward. Mia's hands shook. Despite his declaration that he wanted them to be together, there was a huge difference between building toward a committed relationship and becoming parents.

Well, there was nothing she could do until everyone was gone. Melody was staying at her brother's house while she worked on her album at Ugly Trout Records, and had ridden with them. When Kyle offered to give her a ride home, Mia and Nate exchanged a satisfied look.

It took an hour for Savannah to pry Trent away from the game. Dylan was sacked out in his father's arms and she declared it was time to head home and put him to bed. As the door closed on Savannah, Trent and Dylan, Nate turned to Mia.

"And then there were two," he said, his smile conveying both tenderness and desire.

Mia couldn't resist the invitation in his eyes. She lifted herself onto her toes, but just as her lips made contact with his, her phone buzzed in her back pocket and she instinctively flinched.

"Ignore it," Nate said, gathering her into his arms for a proper kiss that left her gasping for breath and aching for more.

She wrapped her arms around his neck and trembled as he slid his palms beneath her shirt and up along her rib cage to her breasts. Her nipples turned to hard buds as electric impulses sizzled and snapped along her nerve endings.

Her phone buzzed a second time. Nate dragged his mouth from hers and cursed.

"It might be my family," she said, hope tugging at her voice. "Let me check."

"Sure. I'll meet you in the bedroom."

She blew him a flirtatious kiss and went into the family room to shut off the television and close the sliding glass doors that led out to the pool. As she walked, she pulled her phone out and keyed her message app. To her disappointment, the text hadn't come from her family, but Yvonne, Ivy's stylist. The dire message had her clicking on the attached link. A second later, she gasped at what appeared.

For the last forty-eight hours Mia hadn't had time

to pop on to social media to see what her sister had been up to. And it had been a relief to be completely disengaged from all the Ivy drama. Nor had she felt any guilt, mostly because of the way her twin had behaved since the truth had come out about Mia's songwriting.

Now, however, all it took was a single Instagram post and she was right back in the thick of the craziness. Mia stared at the picture on her screen. It was a photo of the contents of a very familiar tote. Hers. Including the positive pregnancy test. Also hers.

When had Ivy taken the picture? The answer came at once. The morning of the AMAs, after the television interview. Ivy had asked Mia to get her some coffee. She'd left her tote behind.

Mia's skin turned to ice. All this time her sister had known? Why hadn't Ivy said anything? Suddenly Mia couldn't breathe.

"Mia?" Nate's voice came from the direction of the master bedroom.

"I'll be there in a second."

Her attention returned to her phone. Suddenly, the screen lit up with her mother's number, but Mia doubted she was reaching out to wish Mia a happy Thanksgiving. She let the call go to voice mail and blocked all incoming calls. Then she went back to staring at the picture.

Before she spoke with anyone, she and Nate needed to have a conversation. Ivy's bid for attention on social media had highlighted that Mia's secret was out of the bag. Was it in retribution for her belief that Mia had spilled Ivy's own secret? If so, why not announce that Mia was pregnant?

Because this created a huge buzz. One that might distract everyone from the songwriting scandal and create confusion about the authenticity of all the latest Ivy Bliss stories.

"Mia?" Nate sounded closer.

She'd sat down at the breakfast bar when the room started spinning. Now she looked up and spied him standing a few feet away.

"Sorry," she murmured, struggling to focus, with her thoughts in turmoil. "Did you say something?"

"I asked if you're okay. You've gone awfully pale."

"I'm…"

It was time to tell Nate that she was pregnant. In truth, she'd already delayed too long. The words were on her lips. She just needed to get them out.

"I'm…"

About to be very, very sick.

When Mia rushed out of the room, Nate picked up the cell phone she'd left behind and looked at the photo on the screen. A positive pregnancy test lay nestled atop a wallet, a familiar shade of lipstick and a teal-colored journal, which was probably the one Ivy had ruined when she threw it into the pool. His brain was slow to process the tableau.

What was Mia doing with a pregnancy test in her purse? From down the hall came the sound of retching. Answers from that quarter weren't going to come as soon as he liked. Nate glanced at the text below the photo. It was not Ivy's feed, but that of her friend Skylar. Nowhere in the description was Mia's name mentioned. The photo was teased with Ivy's name and…his.

Now Nate understood Mia's abrupt flight from the room. Fury exploded inside him. Did she seriously in her wildest imagination think he'd ever touched Ivy? That he would do something so cruel to her? Was this why she'd been acting so strange lately? How long had she thought this of him? Obviously, she'd known her sister was pregnant since before they'd gone to the AMAs. Why hadn't she asked him about it? That she had so little faith in him cut Nate to the core.

And what of Ivy? Nate doubted this little stunt had been accomplished without her approval. She'd never tolerate such betrayal from her posse. He couldn't imagine what this would mean for Mia. Would she see herself even more firmly bound to her sister? Or could this be an opportunity for her to break free of her family?

Before he could ask that question, he needed to sort out what was going on in Mia's head. Nate headed down the hall and found Mia on the floor in his master bathroom. She sat with her back to the soaker tub, knees drawn up to her chest, arms wrapped around her legs. Although she'd doubtless heard his approach, she didn't look up from the floor when he stopped in the doorway.

"Are you okay?"

"No." Despite her stricken expression, the word came out with a sarcastic twist. She pushed to her feet and crossed to the sink. After splashing water on her face, she reached for her toothbrush.

"You know I never slept with Ivy." He paused, waiting for her reaction, and when none came, he continued, "I never touched her, never even looked at her in that way."

Mia closed her eyes and didn't respond. Did she not believe him? Was that really possible, given everything they'd been to each other? Nate joined her at the sink and met her gaze in the mirror. Her only acknowledgment was a slight frown before she bent down to rinse the toothpaste from her mouth.

"Why don't you believe me?"

"I do." A tear trickled down her cheek. Air hissed between her teeth as she dashed it away. "But the fact is, it is your baby."

Nate couldn't believe what she was saying to him. "That's both ridiculous and impossible."

Mia turned to look at him at last. "The piece of the puzzle that you're missing," she said, her voice breaking on the words, "is that the pregnancy test doesn't belong to Ivy."

"If it doesn't belong to her, then…" The impact of understanding was like trying to walk through a closed glass door. He bounced off the invisible surface, his whole body rattled by the impact. "You're pregnant?"

"Yes." She nodded as if for emphasis.

Shock reverberated through him like thunder. "How long?"

"Sydney."

"I meant how long have you known?" A voice in the back of his mind told him this was the best thing that ever happened to him. But it was a quiet reminder, easily drowned out by the anger that licked through him because she'd kept this a secret. "It had to be before Ivy threw your journal in the pool. I saw it beneath the pregnancy test."

"The morning of the AMAs."

"Why didn't you say something?"

Her eyes widened. "It was a huge event for you. I didn't want to ruin…"

When she bit her lip and didn't finish, he jumped in. "Why would you think finding out I was going to be a father would ruin anything?"

She frowned at his aggressive tone. "I didn't plan this. I didn't want you to think I was trying to trap you."

"Trust me, that's the last thing I'd ever think." He gave a bitter laugh. "In fact I'd be overjoyed if that had truly been your motive. At least then I could count on you and me being together."

She didn't immediately respond to his accusation, but a hot burst of color flared across her cheekbones. "That's unfair."

"Is it? You still haven't explained why you didn't tell me as soon as you realized you were pregnant."

"I was scared, okay?"

"Of what? Me?"

"Of everything changing."

"What's so horrible about that?"

"You just don't understand."

But he did. She'd rather remain in her sister's shadow, where she thought it was safe, instead of taking a chance with him.

"When are you going to stop hiding behind Ivy?"

"Hiding? That's not it. You know how she is. What she's struggling with. Every time I'm not there for her something terrible happens."

And there was the core of their problem.

"You can't be your sister's keeper forever." Nate lowered his voice as he fought for calm. "She's never going to take responsibility for herself if you and the rest of your family don't stop enabling her."

"I can't have this conversation again." Mia's lower lip quivered. She caught it between her teeth and pushed away from the sink.

Nate was on her heels as she reentered the master bedroom and made a beeline for the door. He caught her arm and spun her around to face him. "Where are you going?"

"I need some time to think."

"You've had months and months to think. What you need to do is make a decision about us."

She crossed her arms over her chest. "You don't think I know that?"

He stroked his palms up her arms to her shoulders, but made no move to draw her close. "We are having a baby." He emphasized each and every word, hoping to penetrate the wall of stubbornness she erected around herself. "I intend to be in my child's life. And not in a long-distance sort of way." He didn't mean to sound so angry. He loved her. He wanted to be with her. To marry her and raise their child together. Instead he'd declared a challenge, bordering on a threat. "I've asked you to stay in Las Vegas with me. You haven't said yes. So, what's it going to be, Mia?"

"I want to." Her eyes pleaded with him through the tears. "You want me to choose between you and Ivy. I can't do that."

"Are you going to choose between our baby and Ivy?"

He might as well have hit her. She reeled backward two steps and stared at him in dismay. "That's not fair. Our baby comes first."

Our baby. He liked the sound of that. But what about him? Was she going to choose him?

"Look, I'm sorry." It was inadequate, but he made the apology sincere and heartfelt. "Let's sit down and start again, only calmer this time."

Her hands shook as she dragged them through her hair. "Okay."

She let him guide her toward the bed. They settled

onto the mattress with their backs against the head-board and said nothing for a long time.

"I'm sorry." She set her head against his shoulder and reached for his hand.

"For what?"

"This is not at all how I wanted you to find out that you were going to be father."

"It's not how I expected it to happen, either." He gave a soft chuckle. "Actually, I'm not sure I have any idea what I expected."

"Are you really okay with this?"

"So okay." He threaded their fingers together and gave a gentle squeeze. "It's pretty amazing, in fact. Every time my dad came after me when I was a kid I thought about what being a father entailed. Not everyone is cut out for it, but I knew I'd work twice as hard at it to make up for the hell my dad put me through."

"You're going to make an amazing father. We'll figure out everything. I just need some time to talk to my family. It's pretty obvious from the way Ivy is acting out that dealing with her is not going to be easy."

"You don't have to do it alone. Let me be there for you when you go talk to them." He knew better than to suggest he go with her to confront Ivy. Mia knew how to handle her sister better than anyone.

But to announce a false pregnancy on social media and name him as the baby's father was beyond disturbing. Nate swallowed an I-told-you-so.

As much as he wanted to reiterate his opinion on how the entire family's pandering had created the monster that was Ivy Bliss, Mia needed his support, not his criticism.

"Don't be mad," she began, trying for a smile and not succeeding. "I really think I need to go explain things to my dad on my own. Having you there will just complicate the whole situation."

Nate shrugged off his disappointment. He'd like to be at her side, presenting a united front to her father. For support and because he worried that she'd cave to her family once again. "I'll let you handle your family, but I'm telling you right now that I'm calling my publicist and having her deny that your sister and I have had or are having any sort of relationship."

The last thing he intended to do was get into a social media pissing match with Ivy. At least she'd had the sense not to post a picture or the caption herself. She would have plausible deniability.

Suddenly, he was sick to death of talking about Mia's sister. "For the next twelve hours we are not going to talk about a certain pop star. Can you do that?"

"I don't know. I'm not sure I've ever gone that long without talking about her." A cheeky grin spread across Mia's face. "Actually, now that I think about it, there were a couple nights I'll never forget with a handsome guy."

Damn if his pulse didn't kick up a notch. She had the most amazing effect on him. It was what he kept coming back over and over despite how much her obligation to her sister irritated him. But they would worry about her sister later. Right now, it was all about Mia. He eased her back against the headboard and slid his fingers into her hair. She sighed in delight and tilted her face to receive his descending mouth.

Eleven

The next morning, Mia packed a bag and let Nate drive her to the airport to catch a ten o'clock flight to LA, where Ivy and their father were meeting with Trent about the album and their interest in having Hunter Graves produce it instead of Nate.

To her surprise, she hadn't received a single call or text from her family. No doubt they were all in crisis mode over the Instagram post. Mia wondered how her sister was coping with the fallout. Nate had done as he'd promised and released a statement through his publicist. And then he'd watched her fidget as the night stretched on with none of her family reaching out to her.

Was she crazy to resent being shut out after everything she'd sacrificed for her sister and her career?

And then she realized how foolish that sounded. None of her family were avoiding her; more likely they just hadn't bothered to bring her into the loop. Resentment flared.

As he pulled to a stop at the terminal, Nate put his hand on hers and gave a reassuring squeeze. "Are you sure you don't want to just forget about coming clean with your family, and stay with me?"

With each minute that passed she felt less confident about going alone to LA, but she'd put off telling her family about Nate and her pregnancy long enough.

"I appreciate your offer, but I think it will go better if I talk to them in person." She exited the car and waited while Nate pulled her suitcase out of the trunk. "I'll call you later."

But as Mia headed to the counter to check in and drop off her luggage, she was overwhelmed by a mixed bag of emotions. Annoyance. Dread. Her relationship with Nate had been a secret she'd kept to herself for almost four months. Loving him had given her greater joy than anything she'd ever known, and yet she'd hidden her happiness for fear of it being taken away if the truth came out.

It was something she hadn't explained to Nate. He'd assumed that she was afraid of moving forward because her identity was trapped in her sister's shadow. After she'd told him about Ivy's near death experience thanks to the painkillers, he'd been more understanding about the burden of responsibility she felt toward her twin. But he resented that she couldn't leave her sister to make mistakes and face consequences.

Well, Ivy was on her own right now and look what had happened. Hunter Graves was probably going to produce her next album, and while the man was nearly as talented as Nate, Hunter's vision for her music was in line with Ivy's own. They weren't going to record a breakout album. If Ivy had only listened to her...

Mia cut off the thought. Nate was right. She was too caught up in her sister's career and life. Even now, with things so strained between them, even though Ivy had fired her, Mia remained emotionally invested in what her sister was doing.

When it was Mia's turn to step up to the counter, instead of presenting her ticket to LA, she checked to see if there was a flight to Chicago. Suddenly, more than anything, Mia craved some advice from her older sister, Eva. She didn't pause to wonder whether Eva would be happy to see her. Many times in the last five years Eva had also questioned her dedication to Ivy, and as much as they loved each other, Mia's stubborn refusal to leave her twin had led to some tense discussions between Eva and her. Despite this, Mia knew Eva would welcome her with open arms.

After successfully switching her ticket and getting through security, Mia raced to catch her flight and emailed her sister about the surprise visit, mentioning the post on Instagram and offering a brief explanation about the trouble she and Ivy were having. Normally Mia didn't involve Eva in her Ivy issues because she knew how Eva would respond, but Mia wanted her sister's expert opinion.

She had to shut her phone down before Eva replied. Most likely she was in the middle of a session with one of her patients. As a deaf psychiatrist, Eva had a unique niche: almost two thirds of her patients were hearing impaired.

Once she landed in Chicago, Mia exited the airplane and headed for O'Hare's baggage claim. The plan after she collected her luggage was to take the blue line downtown and then the purple line north to her sister's condo in Evanston. The trip would take around an hour and a half. But as Mia entered the baggage claim area she saw a familiar face and sped toward her older sister.

She was so overwhelmed by surprise and relief, she forgot to sign as she blurted, "What are you doing here?" It was the last sentence she uttered before sobs overtook her. Eva's unexpected appearance and the relief of not having to wait two more hours to hug her pulled the cork from the bottle containing Mia's turbulent emotions.

Eva didn't ask questions; she merely wrapped her arms around Mia and let her release all the pent-up sadness that had been building for the last few months. When Mia got herself back under control she realized Eva had coaxed her out of the flow of people and toward the wall. With the initial rush of her tears slowing to a trickle, Mia gave her sister a watery smile.

"What are you doing here?" Mia repeated the question out loud as she wiped her eyes. Eva could read lips and also speak. The sisters usually communicated in a combination of both. "I was going to take the train to your office."

"I canceled my last two appointments," Eva signed. *"You didn't seriously think I was going to let you take the train."*

It seemed impossible that Mia had more tears to shed, but as she and Eva walked arm-in-arm to the baggage claim, Mia's cheeks remained wet. Her initial outburst had lasted long enough for the luggage to make its way from the belly of the airplane to the terminal. Mia collected her suitcase and followed her sister to short-term parking, where she'd left her car.

Because it was impossible for them to have a conversation while Eva drove, they sat in the parking lot long enough for Eva to ask several questions.

"Have you spoken to Ivy and asked her what she was thinking?"

"No. I was afraid what I might say."

"Have you talked to Mom and Dad?"

Again Mia shook her head. "I'm also afraid of what they'll say."

"Do you want to tell me what happened now or wait until we get to my condo?"

"I'll wait."

While Eva drove, she shared with Mia bits of what

had been going on in her job. Although Eva preferred to sign, she'd also learned how to speak. She'd had to in order to communicate with their father and sister, neither of whom had learned more than the most basic of signs. Mia knew this hurt Eva, but she was a pragmatist. Which was why she'd left California to pursue psychiatry. Her life in Chicago was the sort of normal Mia craved.

"Are you hungry?" Eva signed as they waited at the bottom of the freeway ramp for the light to turn green. *"We can go to a restaurant and you can tell me what's going on. Or we can go home."*

Mia grew confused by something in her sister's manner. An evasiveness so unlike Eva that Mia grew immediately suspicious. She had to wait until the next stoplight to ask her question.

"What's going on at home?"

"I thought you might be more comfortable talking without anyone around."

"At a restaurant?" Mia eyed her sister intently. "What's at home that you don't want to bring me there?" Not for one second did Mia think it was anyone from their family, and she knew Nate wasn't aware she'd taken a detour. "Jeremy? Did I interrupt your evening? I'm so sorry."

"Nonsense. I haven't seen you in six months." She shot Mia a wry grin. *"Him I see all the time."*

Eva had been dating Jeremy for the last year. He was a pediatric doctor at Evanston Hospital. They'd met when she'd done her residency there and had been friends for several years before deciding to give dating a try.

Joy flooded Mia. If anyone deserved to be happy it was Eva. "It's gotten serious then?"

The joy shining in Eva's eyes was answer enough. *"We're living together."*

"Wow."

A spike of envy drove through Mia's heart. She didn't resent her sister's happiness, but it shone a light on her own failure to grab the brass ring. Mia's eyes went to Eva's bare left hand as her sister rubbed her ring finger in an unconscious gesture.

"Are you engaged?"

Eva nodded but looked pained. Mia flinched as the subtext hit her in the chest.

"How long?"

"Six weeks. We wouldn't be living together otherwise."

Eva had been engaged for six weeks and had kept it secret from her family. Or perhaps *secret* wasn't the best word. Their parents, Ivy, even Mia, were so focused on Ivy's career that there wasn't room for anything else.

"Where is your ring?"

"My purse."

Mia opened her sister's purse and dug the diamond ring from a zippered interior pocket. She drew it out and handed it to her sister, who slipped it on. "I'm sorry I didn't know."

The stoplight turned green and Eva started the car forward.

"My fault. I should have told you."

But it wasn't Eva's fault. With their lack of interest and support, her family had failed her. It was almost as if once Eva went off to college and then moved to Chicago to do her psychiatric residency she'd been forgotten. Maybe that wasn't completely fair. Mia and their mom flew out to spend long weekends with her a couple times a year. And Eva tried to get back to the West Coast at least once a year, either around the holidays or when Ivy took a break from promoting, recording or touring.

But there was no avoiding the fact that the Navarro family revolved around Ivy and her career.

"Why did you keep it from me?" Even as she asked the question, Mia knew the answer. "Because of what happened to me? Did you think I wouldn't be happy for you because I've royally screwed up with Nate?"

Eva shook her head and Mia saw how her sister's situation was similar to her own. They'd both kept the men they loved from their family in order to savor the joy for as long as possible. It wasn't as if anyone would actively disapprove, but their family had a knack for spoiling things without trying.

"I want to tell him congratulations. Let's go to your condo."

But it turned out that Eva was wrong about her fiancé being at home. He'd left a sweet note explaining that he'd gone out for drinks with his buddies and would catch dinner and be back late. That left hours and hours for the sisters to talk and for Mia to unburden herself.

She started by explaining about how she and Nate had discovered their mutual connection through sign language and then described their secret rendezvous and their one night together in Sydney.

"Very romantic," Eva signed with a hearty sigh.

"And stupid. Looking back, I regret hiding what was happening."

"But you knew Ivy would spoil things."

Mia had known that. *"Why is she like that?"*

"Insecurity. She thinks everyone is happier than she is."

"With all her beauty, fame and success, how is that possible?"

Mia hadn't yet come clean with Eva about being pregnant, and before she could, Jeremy returned home. Mia rushed to congratulate him on convincing the best girl in the world to marry him. By the time they'd finished discussing wedding plans it was late. Both Eva and Jeremy had to be at work early the next morning. They said their good-nights and Mia went to the guest bedroom.

Despite her lack of sleep the night before, Mia was still on Pacific time. Once she'd changed into her sleepwear, she sat wide-eyed and cross-legged on the bed in the beautifully decorated guest room.

She picked up her phone and puzzled over the lack

of messages and emails. And then she realized she'd not taken her phone off airplane mode. She swiftly restored her cell service and watched the red notification indicators explode.

Even before his car cleared the airport, Nate started kicking himself for not accompanying Mia to LA. He never should've let her talk him into staying behind. They were in this together and together was how they should have tackled her father and sister.

If he wasn't so damn busy with the studio he would circle around right this second, drop his car in short-term parking and chase after her. But he had a business to run and artists he couldn't let down. Maybe he could reschedule his day tomorrow and fly to LA tonight. Nate headed for the studio to see what could be done before he let Mia know his plans.

Two hours later he'd spoken with all the artists who were coming in to work with him the next day. Each of them was fine with a short postponement. It meant Nate was going to be working extra-long hours in the days to come, but standing beside Mia as she told her father that she was pregnant was worth it.

Nate called Mia to tell her his plans, but got her voice mail. He'd expected as much. She was probably midflight on her way to LA. She would get the message when she landed and know to put off meeting with her father until later that night.

Pleased with the arrangements he'd made, Nate headed into the studio. He got a text from his publicist letting him know his statement had gone out to news organizations denying that he was the father of Ivy's baby. An hour later his phone lit up with Javier Navarro's number. Nate was in the middle of a recording session and let the call go to voice mail. He knew it would only annoy Mia's father, but Nate wanted to pick the time and place for his conversation with Javier.

Forty-five minutes later he turned the session over to one of his assistants and headed to his office. Nate dialed Javier and braced himself for what was to come. Ivy's dad could be hotheaded when it came to his daughter.

"How dare you call my daughter a liar," was the first thing out of Javier's mouth.

Nate sighed and pinched the bridge of his nose. "I think you need to have a conversation with your daughter," he said. "I am not the father of Ivy's baby."

"She says you are."

"That's impossible, since she and I don't have that sort of relationship." Nate wanted very badly to tell Javier exactly what he thought of his spoiled, childish daughter, but he owed it to Mia to try to keep from exacerbating an already tricky situation.

"That's not how she sees it."

Nate was over trying to keep his cool and remain polite, but recognized if he blew up Mia would catch the brunt of the trouble. "Look." He paused to suck in a calming breath and even out his tone. "Ivy and

I never… I don't know why she picked me, but I'm not the guy."

"What reason would my daughter have to lie about something like that?"

"I really couldn't say." He was really trying not to go there with Javier. Nate leaned back in his chair and stared at the ceiling. "I think your daughter is incredibly talented and has the potential to be a huge star. Our relationship is and always has been professional."

"Not all that professional. You've done nothing but badger Ivy the entire time she was recording at your studio."

"That's not what happened." But Nate knew he was wasting his breath. Still, he persisted. "Ivy and I had creative differences, that's all."

"Well, Ivy wants Hunter Graves to step in as the producer."

"Trent and I have already spoken about this and I understand." Nate didn't add that he'd thrown Hunter at Ivy hoping for this exact result. "I'm sure they'll work well together."

"She has a lot riding on this album," Javier said. "I hope the label is ready to get behind her."

"Of course. Ivy is very important to West Coast Records. The intention is to get behind her one hundred percent."

This last seemed to mollify Ivy's father and the conversation ended more cordially than it had begun.

After Nate hung up with Mia's father, he raked his fingers through his hair and spent several minutes calming down. He couldn't call Mia, given his mood. When he felt sufficiently chilled, he dialed her number. Once again it went to voice mail. He left her a quick message, summarizing his conversation with her father. And then he returned to the recording studio to wait for her to call him back.

That call didn't come until a little after nine. He'd just let himself into his hotel room in LA and was about to leave Mia another text when she called.

"Hi."

"Hey." Air gusted from his lungs. He was so relieved to hear her voice. "Did you get my messages?"

"Ah…" She drew the word out. "Not until just now. I'm sorry."

Nate reined in his concern. She sounded mortified, but her voice lacked the tense edge from that morning. He realized that whatever she'd been up to, she'd discovered some peace.

"I cleared my schedule and came to LA. Where are you?"

"Ah…" Again that strange little pause. "I'm not in LA. Last minute, I decided to visit Eva in Chicago."

"That's not what we discussed this morning."

"I know, but I just needed a little more time to think things through and Eva has always been the voice of sanity in our family."

Nate was torn between frustration, relief and concern. Frustration, because he wanted Mia's priorities to shift from her family to him. What would it have taken for her to text him before her flight and let him know where she was bound? But he wasn't going to react as her family would, pushing her around, telling her what she should and shouldn't do.

He was relieved because when he hadn't heard from her since dropping her at the airport, he'd begun thinking all sorts of terrible things. Didn't she realize she meant the world to him, even before he found out she was carrying his child? Why was it she refused to believe anyone would want to put her first? Surely it couldn't all be laid at Ivy's feet.

And lastly he felt concern because if she'd fled to Chicago instead of confronting her problems and going to LA, then she was a lot more out of sorts than she'd let on.

"What did Eva tell you?" Nate made his voice as calm as possible.

"Nothing that I didn't already know. That Ivy is insecure and has a knack for spoiling other people's happiness."

"So what are you going to do about that?"

"Be happy in spite of her?"

"You don't sound very convinced."

"What is wrong with me?" Mia blurted out.

He wished he was there to offer her support, but as he'd often remarked about Ivy needing to become more responsible, Mia also needed to not only claim her independence, but also accept that she deserved to be happy.

"There's nothing wrong with you. It isn't your fault that your parents put too great a burden on you at such a young age. They pushed Ivy to be a star and made you her keeper." Nate paused and listened, wishing he could see Mia face. "There's nothing wrong with you," he repeated, more quietly this time. "Tomorrow you'll fly back to LA, and then you and I will go talk to your parents together."

"Okay." It was a squeaky whisper, as if something was blocking her voice.

"I have your back."

"Thank you." She sounded clearer and more confident.

"You don't have to thank me. It's time someone took care of you. And from now on that someone is me."

Her laughter was the most wonderful thing he'd heard all day. He wished he was there to see happiness brighten her eyes and soften the curve of her lips.

"You know I love you, right?"

She tossed out the phrase with such an ease that he wasn't sure if she meant it as a heartfelt pledge or if they were just words that conveyed her fondness. She still hadn't committed to moving to Las Vegas to be with him. And instead of going to LA to confront her family, she'd run off to Chicago.

"I do now," he teased back, but his heart was a brick in his chest. "Get some sleep. I'll see you tomorrow."

Nate's presence was a solid comfort at her side as Mia pushed the doorbell of Ivy's house the next afternoon. It felt weird to not just let herself in. She'd lived here with Ivy for nearly two years, coming and going at will. But it had never been her home, and since Ivy had tossed her out four days earlier, it didn't feel right to just walk in.

Clara answered the door. The housekeeper gave Mia a tentative smile as she stepped back to let them in, but sadness overcame her features as Mia's eyes fell on the stack of boxes in the foyer.

"I'm so sorry. She made me pack up all your things."

Mia gave the woman a hug. "It's okay." The pile was small enough to fit into their rental SUV: just her clothes, her journals and a few mementos. It was a sad reflection on Mia's personal life to this point.

"How is Ivy doing?"

With a furtive glance over her shoulder, Clara shook her head. "She's…"

"Mia?" Javier Navarro stood at the far end of the foyer, radiating impatience and disapproval. "We're waiting for you in the living room."

Nate squeezed her shoulder and Mia gave Clara a reassuring smile. As the housekeeper stepped aside, Mia lifted her chin. Then, fortified by Nate's support, she headed toward her father. Javier's eyes flickered from her to Nate.

"I don't think it's a good idea that he's here."

"We have something to tell you." Mia's stomach was a knot of anxiety as she and Nate entered the living room. Only her mother occupied the space. "Where's Ivy?"

"She doesn't want to see you," her mother said.

Mia frowned. "I imagine she doesn't want to face up to what she's done."

"And what is that, exactly?" Javier asked, stepping to his wife's side.

"Lied about being pregnant for one." Mia wasn't surprised at her parents' relief. A baby wouldn't be good for Ivy's career. "It was my test she splashed all over social media." Mia glanced up at Nate. "We're going to have a baby."

Mia's mother gasped. "Why would she do that?"

Her spirits plummeted at her mother's words. She'd just announced the most amazing thing that had ever happened to her, but all her parents could think about was Ivy. Her throat tightened.

"It's a cry for help."

"Then you should be here to help her," Javier said.

Beside her, Mia felt Nate tense as the familiar scene played out. "She doesn't want me around anymore," Mia explained.

"I take it back." A soft voice spoke up from the glass doors leading out to the pool. Ivy stood just outside. Wearing workout clothes and no makeup, she looked fragile, unsure and younger than her twenty-five years. "I don't want you to leave me."

Mia glanced over her shoulder at Nate and saw his dismay. He was her future. She couldn't imagine her life any other way. But Ivy was her twin and she couldn't go with Nate until she'd made peace with her.

"Let me go talk to her," Mia said, her gaze lingering on his as she silently pleaded with him to understand.

A muscle worked in his jaw, and then he nodded to the boxes beside the front door. "I'll take those out to the SUV."

Before he could go, Mia stepped into his space and wrapped her arms around his waist. "I love you," she said, her cheek pressed against his chest.

His arms bound her to him until she could barely breathe. "I love you, too."

The words made her smile. She pulled back and looked up at him. "And I'm choosing you."

The relief on his face made her heart stop. He set his forehead against hers. "Thank you." With a quick, hard kiss he let her go. "I'll wait for you outside."

Ignoring her parents, Mia ran across the room and put her arms around Ivy. At first her sister resisted, then her body went limp and she hugged back.

"Don't leave me," Ivy murmured again, her voice muffled against Mia's shoulder.

"You know I have to go. I love Nate. I can't live without him."

"I can't do any of this without you."

"You can and you will. Stop letting Dad pressure you into doing things. Fire him if you have to. Ditch Skylar and Riley. Get clean. Forget about the stupid album. Start a fashion line. Do what you want. I'll support you."

"I'm so sorry about how I treated you."

"I know." As she hugged Ivy she felt as if she got her sister back.

"I'm glad you and Nate are together."

"That means a lot to me."

"We never hooked up, you know."

"I do."

"He's only ever had eyes for you. I saw that while we were on tour and I was so afraid he would take you away from me. But in the end I knew that you needed to go." Ivy gave her a sad smile. "That's why I leaked that you wrote all my songs. I needed a reason to fire you."

Mia was stunned. "You did that?" Her throat closed up. "For me?"

"I knew you wouldn't stop worrying about me."

"But you just asked me to stay."

"I didn't realize how lonely it would be not having you around." Ivy dashed tears from her cheeks. "Now, get out of here before I stop being nice and go all Ivy Bliss on your ass."

Mia laughed. "I love you."

"And I love you."

With one final hug, Mia left her sister and retraced her steps through the living room. She gave her parents a brief nod and burst through Ivy's front door, feeling free for the first time in eight years.

Nate waited for her by the SUV, his tall figure relaxed as she sped across the distance between them. His broad smile became her whole world as she flung herself into his arms and kissed him.

"Let's get out of here." Taking her by the hand,

he led her to the car, opened the passenger door and ushered her inside. Seconds later he was sliding behind the wheel and starting the engine.

"Where are we going?"

"To the shipping store for these boxes, and then the airport. I intend to get you settled in Las Vegas before you change your mind."

"I'm not going to do that," she assured him.

An hour later they were walking hand in hand toward the security checkpoint at LAX when Nate pulled her out of the traffic flow. She gazed up at him in surprise as he gave her a sheepish grin.

"This isn't at all how I'd planned to do this, but it occurs to me they're going to make me empty my pockets." He pulled out a small box and popped the lid. Nestled in the black velvet was a diamond ring. "Mia Navarro, love of my life, will you marry me?"

Stunned to silence, she stared at the gorgeous ring and then lifted her gaze to his.

When she didn't speak, his brows drew together. "I'm not asking because you're pregnant. I'm not that guy."

"You are exactly that guy." She gave a self-conscious laugh. "Which is why I love you."

The look on his face set her heart to pounding. "Say that again," he demanded.

"Say what?"

"That you love me."

"I love you."

"And," he prompted.

"And I absolutely will marry you."

He took her hand in his and slid the ring onto her finger. "You are my world."

Mia put her palm against his cheek and leaned close. "You are mine. Forever and always."

And after a tender kiss that sealed their vows, they headed for the plane that would take them home.

* * * * *

If you liked this story of romance in Vegas pick up these other LAS VEGAS NIGHTS *novels from Cat Schield*

THE BLACK SHEEP'S SECRET CHILD
AT ODDS WITH THE HEIRESS
A MERGER BY MARRIAGE
A TASTE OF TEMPTATION

And don't miss these other great reads by Cat Schield

THE NANNY TRAP
ROYAL HEIRS REQUIRED

Available now from Harlequin Desire!

***

If you're on Twitter, tell us what you think of Harlequin Desire! #harlequindesire

#2527 THE BABY FAVOR

Billionaires and Babies • by Andrea Laurence

CEO Mason Spencer and his wife are headed for divorce when an old promise changes their plans. They are now the guardians for Spencer's niece...and they must remain married. Will this be their second chance, one that leads to forever?

#2528 LONE STAR BABY SCANDAL

Texas Cattleman's Club: Blackmail • by Lauren Canan

When sexy former rodeo champion turned billionaire Clay Everett sets his sights on his spunky secretary, he's sure he holds the reins in their affair. Until he learns Sophie Prescott is carrying his child. Now all bets are off!

#2529 HIS UNEXPECTED HEIR

Little Secrets • by Maureen Child

After a fling with a sexy marine leaves Rita pregnant, her attempts to reach the billionaire are met with silence...until now! Brooding, reclusive Jack offers to marry Rita—in name only. Will his new family give him the heart to embrace life—and love—again?

#2530 PREGNANT BY THE BILLIONAIRE

The Locke Legacy • by Karen Booth

Billionaire Sawyer Locke only makes commitments to his hotel empire—until he meets fiery PR exec Kendall Ross. Now he can't get her out of his mind—or out of his bed. But when she becomes pregnant, will he claim the heir he never expected?

#2531 BEST FRIEND BRIDE

In Name Only • by Kat Cantrell

CEO Jonas Kim must stop his arranged marriage—by arranging a marriage for himself! His best friend, Vivian, will be his wife and never fall in love, or so he thinks. Can he keep his heart safe when Viv tempts him to become friends with benefits?

#2532 CLAIMING THE COWGIRL'S BABY

Red Dirt Royalty • by Silver James

Rancher Kaden inherited a birth father, a powerful last name and wealth—none of which he wants. His pregnant lover, debutante Pippa Duncan, has lost everything due to a dark family secret. Their marriage of convenience may undo the pain of their families' pasts, but will it lead to love?

*When billionaire boss Cameron McNeill goes
undercover in a tropical paradise to check out his
newest hotel's employees, he doesn't expect to want to
claim beautiful concierge Maresa Delphine and her
surprise baby as his own...*

Read on for a sneak peek at
HIS ACCIDENTAL HEIR
by Joanne Rock

As soon as he banished the hotel staff, including Maresa
Delphine, he'd find a quiet spot on the beach where he
could recharge.

Maresa punched a button on the guest elevator while
a young man disappeared down another hall with the
luggage. Cameron's gaze settled on the bare arch of her
neck just above her jacket collar. Her thick brown hair
had been clipped at the nape, ending in a silky tail that
curled along one shoulder. A single pearl drop earring
was a pale contrast to the rich brown of her skin.

She glanced up at him. Caught him staring.

The jolt of awareness flared hot and unmistakable. He
could tell she felt it, too. Her pupils dilated a fraction,
dark pools with golden rims. His heartbeat slugged
heavier. Harder.

He forced his gaze away as the elevator chimed to
announce their arrival on his floor. "After you."

He held the door as she stepped out into the short hall. Cameron used the key card to unlock the suite, not sure what to expect. So far, Maresa had proven a worthy concierge. That was good for the hotel. Less favorable for him, perhaps, since her high standards surely precluded acting on a fleeting elevator attraction.

"If everything is to your satisfaction, Mr. Holmes, I'll leave you undisturbed while I go make your dinner reservations for the week." She hadn't even allowed the door to close behind them, a wise practice, of course, for a female hotel employee.

The young man he'd seen earlier was already in the hall behind her with the luggage cart. Cameron could hear her giving the bellhop instructions.

"Thank you." Cameron turned his back on her to stare out at the view of the hotel's private beach and the brilliant turquoise Caribbean Sea. "For now, I'm satisfied."

The room, of course, was fine. Ms. Delphine had passed his first test.

But satisfied? No.

He wouldn't rest until he knew why the guest reviews of the Carib Grand Hotel were less positive than anticipated. And satisfaction was the last thing he was feeling when the most enticing woman he'd met in a long time was off-limits.

That attraction would be difficult to ignore when it was imperative he uncover all her secrets.

Don't miss
HIS ACCIDENTAL HEIR by Joanne Rock,
available June 2017 wherever
Harlequin® Desire books and ebooks are sold.

www.Harlequin.com